Rowena Evans grew up in an artistic family in Sydney and has always been interested in telling stories and making pictures. As a child she thought all adults were good at drawing and that art and writing were normal occupations. She has a BA in Visual Arts and has worked as an illustrator, printmaker, writer, fairy, cartoonist and in community art, among other things.

Rowena's writing and art contain a mixture of reality and fantasy; it is always possible that something out of the ordinary may appear just around the next corner. Her hobbies include music, wandering about, reading and weeding.

SWITCH

BY
ROWENA EVANS

Sequel to Drums and Power Lines

Switch

ISBN-13: 978-1-922856-54-8

Printed in Garamond and Astrid Long.

IFWG Publishing International
Gold Coast

www.ifwgpublishing.com

For my mother, Halcyon, who taught me to love poetry, books and art, and to look for possibilities.

THE STORY SO FAR IN
DRUMS & POWER LINES

At the start of *Drums & Power Lines,* Ivan is confronted by angry, aggressive Phil after a tumultuous day. Ivan, suddenly finding himself oddly disoriented, meets Cassie, a wild-looking girl. She takes him home to her family's shack. More and more confused, Ivan finds himself in a world that in many ways is the same as his own, while being at the same time profoundly different. He becomes involved in Cassie's search for her missing brother, Pip.

Meanwhile Ivan's older sister Reenie meets the enigmatic Cal, and falls head over heels for his melancholy charm (and auburn hair). Cal is actually Cassie's missing brother, and Ivan's nemesis Phil; Pip being a family nickname, Cal his actual name and Phil the name he has adopted more recently. Reenie and Cal get into his world, only to find turmoil in the town, Willowvale. Cassie and Ivan have been kidnapped by a bikie gang from the nearby city, O'Malley, and Cal and Cassie's parents are involved in dangerous resistance to the oppressive local government. Meanwhile, Cassie and Ivan meet the junior bikie, Wilfred, who isn't as tough as he looks but tougher than he seems. He helps them in their search for Pip.

At the end of *Drums and Power Lines* Wilfred, Cassie and Cal have helped Reenie and Ivan return to their own world by means of being at a particular place, at sunset, while drums are sounding in both worlds. Cal and Reenie are heartbroken to be separated, Ivan and Wilfred both have a crush on Cassie, and Wilfred's rather unpredictable mother Berenice is not having a bar of any more bad behaviour.

The sequel starts at the next moment…

CHARACTERS

who were previously introduced in *Drums and Power Lines,* in order of mention in *Switch*

Cassie

At the beginning of *Drums and Power Lines* Cassie found Ivan, lost and confused, near her home in Willowvale. She is 16 years old at the start of *Switch*.

Thistle & Raven

Cassie's parents. They make a living by making musical instruments and performing, previously clandestinely, but from the beginning of *Switch*, openly, due to changes in their world at the end of *Drums and Power Lines*.

Jess

Older than Cassie and the daughter of the ex-president of Willowvale, the corrupt and contemptible Rex Bagshaw, Jess in the earlier story was an unknown quantity. She and Rex left Willowvale when Rex's machinations were finally exposed and opposed.

Ivan

From the version of Willowvale that exists separately, similar to but different from Cassie's Willowvale, Ivan is the same age as Cassie. His accidental entry into the alternate Willowvale precipitated the adventures of the previous story. Ivan's world is the one from which the reader is viewing the stories.

Wilfred

About the same age as Cassie and Ivan, Wilfred lives in the nearby city of O'Malley. Despite his conservative appearance and mixture of hot temper and caution, Wilfred has qualities of courage and friendship (and a passion for motorbikes) that quickly made him a valued friend to both Cassie and Ivan during the earlier story.

Pip/ Cal/ Phil/ Radcliffe

Cassie's older brother, aged about 18 at the beginning of this story. Pip is his family nickname; Cal is short for his real name, which he does not tell to everyone. In certain circumstances he calls himself Phil or Radcliffe because he's a mysterious character and likes to be confusing and enigmatic. A year before the story of *Drums and Power Lines*, Cal ran away from Willowvale and was not seen by his family until the exciting events of the earlier story reached their conclusion.

Magda and Wolfie

Cassie's family's dogs.

Reenie

Ivan's older sister, about the same age as Cal. In the previous story, Reenie met Cal in her own world, and when they worked out how to get Cal back into his own world, followed him there, almost by accident.

John, Jules and Isabella

Residents of the outer limits of Cassie's Willowvale, John and his partner Jules, and their baby Isabella were previously self-appointed outcasts known as ferals, living outside the walls and rules of the town. John is unpredictable and Jules tough.

Berenice

Wilfred's mother. He has never met his father. Berenice has brought Wilfred up in a tasteful home with many rules and expectations. She works hard, but her capricious and manipulative behaviour is probably the cause of Wilfred's surprising streak of rebelliousness.

Mum, Dad and Anna

Ivan and Reenie's parents Mick and Elena Williams, and younger sister, aged about 11 at the time of this story.

Gran & Pop/old Mrs & Mr Williams

Ivan and Reenie's grandparents—Mick's parents. They exist in both versions of Willowvale, as do some other characters.

Mick and Penny Williams

Both Mick and Penny exist in both worlds. Mick is Ivan and Reenie's father in their world: Penny and Mick are married to each other, with completely different lives, in Cassie's world. In Ivan's world, Penny is a friend of his parents.

Sinclair
A member of the motorcycle gang, The Gentlemen of the Road, Sinclair is previously known to Cal, Wilfred, Cassie and Ivan.

Frankie
Ivan's family's dog.

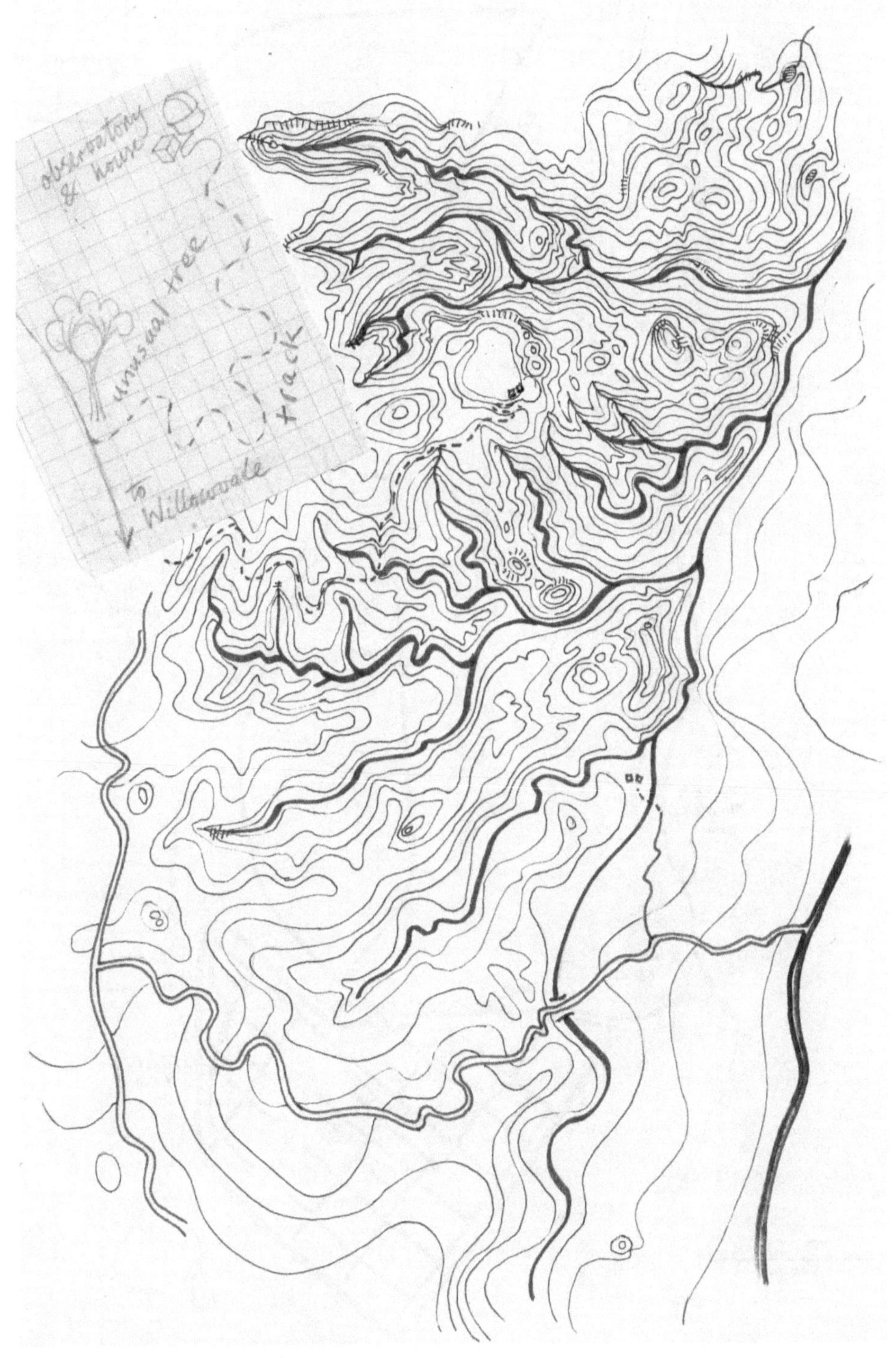

observatory
& house
unusual tree
track
to Willowvale

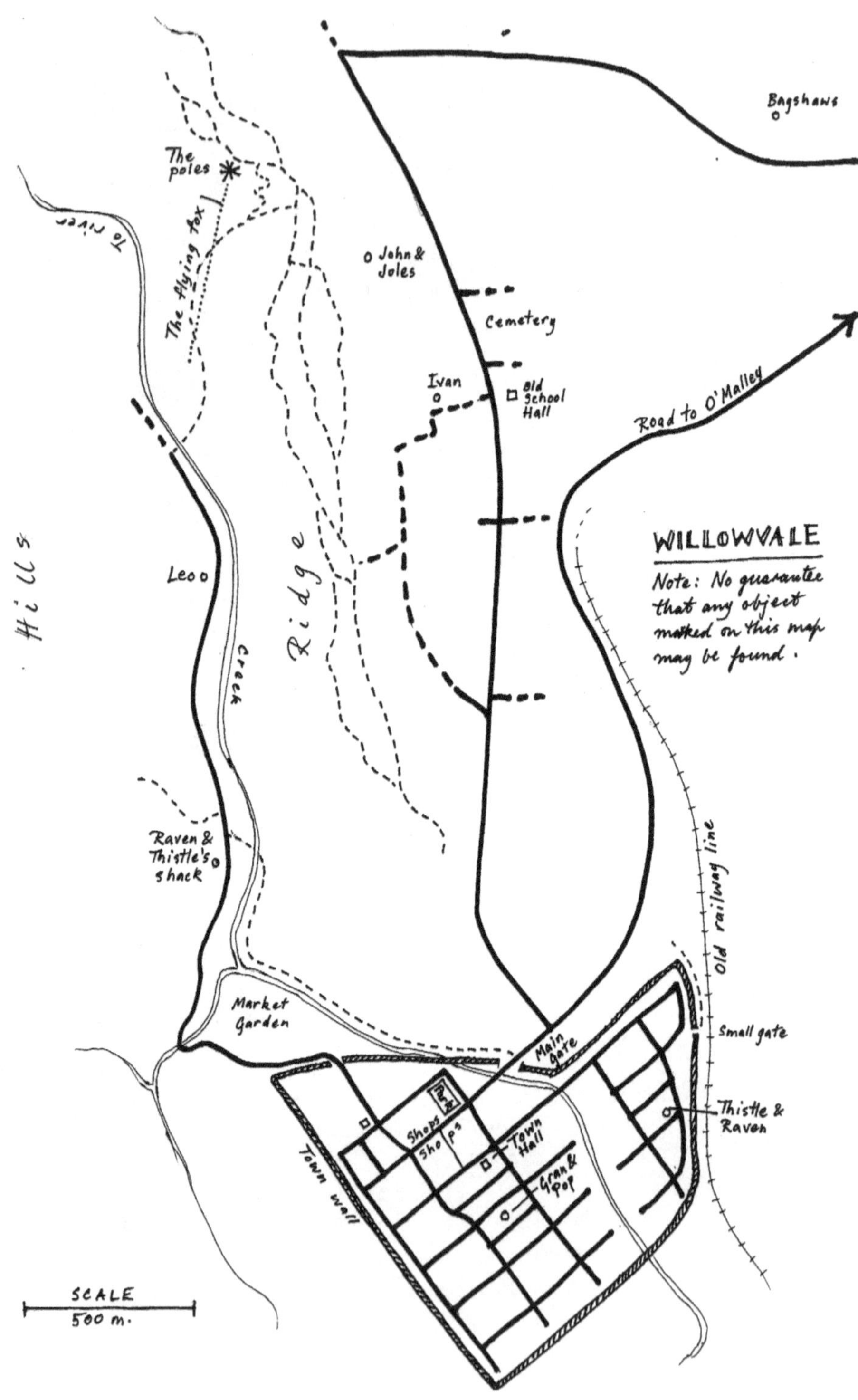

Bagshaws
The poles
The flying fox
To River
o John & Joles
Cemetery
Ivan
Old School Hall
Road to O'Malley
WILLOWVALE
Note: No guarantee that any object marked on this map may be found.
Hills
Leo
Ridge
Creek
Raven & Thistle's shack
Old railway line
Market Garden
Small gate
Main gate
Thistle & Raven
Shops
Shops
Town Hall
Gran & Pop
Town wall
SCALE
500 m.

CHAPTER ONE

PIP

Thursday afternoon. Cassie stared at a page of the textbook, her mind wandering. She knew what she was feeling. A subtle change from normal, or the way "normal" had been lately, to a strange disquiet—to something like a conscious worry niggling at a corner of her mind. Her parents, Thistle and Raven, were in their workshop happily working on new musical instruments. Sounds of filing and sawing, and the comforting smell of sawdust and lacquer floated through the open window. Cassie's thoughts floated with the sawdust. She turned a page of the book. School, though not her favourite place to be, had become a lot more bearable since the events of last winter. It wasn't just that Jess had gone (though that was certainly a big improvement) but the way almost everything was better since then. Cassie thought back as she had many times to when everything changed. The most exciting day.

"No. It started before that," she said out loud as if to correct her thoughts. Which day from that week was really the most exciting? The last one, when the whole of Willowvale finally got some sense and rebelled against that horrible tin pot ruler, Bagshaw? That was the day when things really changed for the better for everyone; the day when pointless rules disappeared like the fading of the exhaust smoke from the tail of Rex Bagshaw's flashy car. The day music was allowed back into the open, and people could travel to O'Malley whenever they wished. And when so many other things that had been odd and annoying melted away. That last day was exciting, it was true. But the real changes in her life began earlier than that.

There was not a day in the last six months when Cassie had not thought about the strange arrival of Ivan. Ivan, appearing on the rocks at the top of the flying fox, from nowhere. His strange ignorance, his odd confusion that the world was different from how it should be. His ability to be annoying, while at the same time brave and truthful. The way her opinion of him had changed in the week they had known each other.

But no. The real change in her life had started more than a year before that; the day Pip ran away. It was that day that Cassie had the same uneasy feeling—now it came back to her like a shock. Pip not home from school (whether he actually went there or not, her parents did not know) at the usual time. Not home from hanging 'round town with his friends. Not home from an evening at the Bagshaw's tasteless O'Malley-style house getting up to goodness knows what with Jess and the others in their gang. Not home at all. Cassie found herself staring unseeing at the page of her textbook. It was the same now. He was late home every night.

It was still hot. Cassie poured herself a glass of water from the jug and went out to the front step. The sun was already low above the hill behind the house. Evenings were deceptive at this time of year, and her parents were working late. The changes in town meant everyone wanted music now, and Thistle and Raven with their still-new delight in being able to work openly, and perform music any time they wanted, were busy in their workroom. She heard their voices, sometimes one asking the other to pass a tool, sometimes one or both of them breaking into a hummed tune. If she wanted to eat she had better light the fire and pick some vegetables from the garden; but first, with that vague unease about Pip, she needed a walk to clear her head.

Cassie patted her thigh and whistled for the dogs, but they just lifted their big heads and looked at her. Why walk when they could lie in the shade?

"I'll go down to the creek," Cassie said, picked up a bucket to make herself feel purposeful, and headed down the track to the road that led through the valley, between the town and the bottom of the ridge where she had first met Ivan.

At the point where the path met the road, Cassie paused. There was a lot more traffic here since the town walls were opened up and the restrictions broken down. Pip's job had contributed to the traffic, with the introduction of motor vehicles and new bicycles, and everything with wheels. One or two people had even bought shiny motorbikes from O'Malley, which Pip had a knack for fixing when they broke down. The local blacksmith had pretty much begged him to work for him. Cassie wasn't so sure about the vehicles. They were noisy, smelly and moved too fast. She always stopped at the point where the house track met the road, in case one was speeding round the bend—not that she wouldn't hear it coming. To tell the truth, she was a little scared of them, still. Their smell and roar reminded her of that horrible moment outside the old school hall when she'd been surrounded and thrown onto the back of one like a sack of oats. The moment when Ivan risked everything to help her. She shook herself.

That was odd. She saw Pip. He was walking away, already past the house. What was he doing?

"Pip! Where are you going?" He ignored her, or was too far away to hear.

It was difficult having Pip for a brother. Sometimes Cassie wondered what it would be like to have a different brother, a calmer, easier brother like Wilfred or even Ivan; though it was tricky, for some reason, to imagine Wilfred with his smooth blonde hair and neat ways as a brother, and virtually impossible to imagine Ivan as one, except to his real sisters. She decided they were better as friends, even if she was never going to see Ivan again, and hadn't heard from Wilfred. Ivan had his own sisters, and Wilfred, as far as she knew, was an only child, with that awful mother. Cassie hurried after Pip, full of curiosity. She sometimes thought her memory of him before he ran away was false, because she remembered him as being completely different from the way he was now. He'd always been what her parents called *intense*, and she had to admit that the couple of months before he ran away were filled with conflict and tension. Now, although everyone was overjoyed to have him back, and although there was none of the charged atmosphere that had previously existed between him and their parents, Pip was silent and distant, always staring to the hills as if expecting something to happen. But, Cassie thought, even if his shiny image in her mind had been a little dented by recent events, she still loved him so much it almost hurt.

Cassie dropped the bucket with a clang. Pip was far down the road now, walking very fast. Cassie's bare feet were tough but it was difficult to keep up, and impossible to gain on him. She heard her mother come to the door and call for her. "I'll be back before they miss me properly," she thought as she strode after Pip. "I wish I'd brought the dogs." Their long legs would have meant they caught and delayed him so she could easily catch up.

Pip continued fast. He reached the blackberry-tangled ford at the end of the road. Cassie, still far behind, lost sight of him until she reached the same place and saw his footprints in the muddy ground. She pushed through the narrow gap in the thicket, thorns pulling at her hair and arms. Ow. Trod on one. Out in the open, from the bottom of the old flying fox apparatus, she saw him enter the steep gully that led to the top of the ridge. Shadow climbed the valley wall. Cassie felt uneasy. The sunset curfew—

Oh. Even after six months it was still ingrained. To be home inside the walls when the sunset signal drums sounded. That was all finished now, she knew, but it was difficult to forget. The last drums sounded the day Ivan and Reenie left. She knew they were the last. She knew Ivan and Reenie were gone forever. She had helped them go, helped them return to their home that was just over the ridge but in a completely different world to which she would never go. She saw them disappear to that world at the moment when the sun fell behind the western trees, as the drums played.

The thought of that sunset flashed an image into Cassie's mind with clarity that hadn't been there at the time. She saw the scene again, lit in orange light, blue shadows not creeping but surging up the valley wall, the sun falling unstoppably to the horizon, Wilfred banging on the curfew drum as if his life depended on it. She saw herself and Ivan hugging each other, knowing they'd never meet again and not knowing how to feel, nor wanting to think about it. She remembered feeling his bones creak, so tightly she grasped him, reluctant to let him go after all they'd been through together. She remembered…

Cassie blushed at her own obtuseness. She remembered Pip and Reenie standing, metres apart, but linked by the same bleak expression of impending loss. How could she have been so perfectly stupid? She'd seen them together that day when everyone found each other. Now she understood his plan.

"Pip! Wait!" The track was rough and it was a hot afternoon. Cassie ran. "Pip!" she panted. She stubbed her toe on a rock but struggled on, up the steep hill, ignoring pain. Her hair stuck to her sweaty face. A kookaburra called nearby, frightening her for a moment, reinforcing her feeling of foolishness. The shadow of the opposite ridge climbed the hill ahead of her, always out of reach, taking the colour of the day with it.

Then the drum started.

"It's impossible. No, he can't leave again. It's not happening." She almost fell up the last few metres of the track, and, stumbling over rocks and logs, flew through the sudden summer twilight over the short distance to the place.

Feral John sat on a rock, hitting the skin of the old curfew drum hard with a stick, again and again.

"Stop!" shrieked Cassie and threw herself at him. "Pip. Where's Pip?" She cannonballed into John with all her strength and the impact knocked the drum out of his grasp. It rolled and bounded off the rock on which John sat. Cassie heard it crash through vegetation and land with a sickening boom and crash, far below.

"You've done it now," said John with smug reproach. Cassie's blow had had no other effect on his solid mass than the loss of the drum.

"You've done it, you've done it," screamed Cassie, hitting out at John, who deflected her with careless ease. "Where's Pip?"

"You know full well where he is. And not comin' back now, thanks to you."

"You idiot. How could you? What will Thistle and Raven do? He's only been home a few months."

"He went to see that young lady he was so taken with. He was pining. Wasn't going to be happy until—"

"Of course he was happy, you wombat-arsed fool."

"Nothin' wrong with wombats," said John, to nobody in particular. "Got to be going. Jules is waiting."

"How's he going to get back?" She should have guessed what Pip was planning.

"You might fix it if you're lucky," John said over his shoulder as he walked away. Cassie looked over the brink of the rock. In the dimness she saw scattered splinters of pale curved wood and rags of the shredded drum skin. The drum was ruined and it was all her fault.

The flying fox hung at the top pole. It was a rule to haul it back up the cable by a very long trace rope at the bottom or top, after you'd used it. Now that it wasn't needed for emergency travel to the valley for whatever emergencies they used to be meant to believe in, it was used for fun by local kids. Cassie suspected that Thistle and Raven used it occasionally, too, after their music rehearsals at the old school hall, though she found it quite difficult to imagine her stern, purposeful parents doing anything except playing music, for fun. It beat walking all the way back, though. She unhooked the rope that held it and tested the cable. Lucky she hadn't brought Magda and Wolfie after all. No. Nothing about this pointless chase was lucky. Pip was gone back to Reenie and Ivan's world. There was no way of getting him back. None. He was gone forever. She'd never see him again. There was no hope. How could anything about it be called lucky? She might be lucky if the cable failed and she was flung to the ground. Then she wouldn't have to explain to her parents. On this gloomy thought Cassie twisted her hand securely into the strap and leapt off the platform. Tears blurred her vision as she flew down the cable toward the valley.

CHAPTER TWO
QUESTIONS

"Wait till your father hears about this. You were such a good little boy. What's happened to you?"

Wilfred wasn't at all worried about the threat. His mother was playing her drama queen role again. He hadn't seen his father for so long that he couldn't remember what he looked like. Indeed, sometimes he wondered whether he was still alive, or in his wilder moments whether he even existed. But the thing Wilfred wondered about most was whether he really knew his mother. Her behaviour was certainly difficult to comprehend.

"You haven't seen my father for years. How would you know what he thinks? He has no right to tell me what to do. He obviously doesn't care." None of these responses were spoken. Wilfred knew better than that. Although at times he didn't understand his mother at all, he knew the pointlessness of arguing with her, and that the only way to do what he wanted was to simply do it. His mistake this time had been getting caught leaving the house. He zipped up his jacket and put his perso-text into his pocket.

Berenice slammed her mug onto the kitchen bench and burst into tears. "You don't know how difficult it is being a single parent."

Wilfred heard, but he was already out the door. He did sort of understand. He did know how hard she worked to keep them both in the nice house with nice furniture and a shiny kitchen full of gadgets. But being the only child of a single parent wasn't easy either. Why did she have to make things so hard for him too? Why? And he was still a good kid in almost every way. That was, he thought as he stomped down the front steps, the cause of most of his problems.

The motorcycle engine gave its best impression of a roar into life— the best it could at 175 ccs. Wilfred revved the engine loudly—before he put it into gear—to relieve his stress, buckled the catch on his helmet, which matched the bike (in some respects he was more his mother's child than he liked to admit), checked the fuel gauge and drove away from the pastel-coloured house where his mother wanted him to live a neat, pastel-coloured life exactly the way she planned it. Houses flashed past, their colours blending in his peripheral vision to a gelato blur like melting ice cream.

Why had he left this trip for so long? What had he been waiting for? Months and months. Cassie hadn't written or sent a message of any kind. The pain of waiting was a dull weight inside him. Maybe that weight itself had discouraged him from acting. The burden that tainted school, his reactions to his mother, his relationships with the aunties, uncles and cousins who were his next closest family. Why hadn't he just got on the bike and gone to see her before? His job at the sundae shop? It was easy enough to change shifts with somebody else. School? Well, that was only a few hours four days a week. Berenice? Wilfred revved the engine again and sped towards Willowvale.

The road as far as the resort had always been good. Flags fluttered from the hotel roof and in the car park, and screams of enjoyment or fear came from the World's Largest Waterslide, which took thrill-seekers from the top of the crater to the cold waters of the lake. Wilfred stopped at the lookout to calm himself. Yachts drifted on the water, all leaning in unison like dancers as the breeze caught their sails. The sun was still high above the craggy wooded hills across the old river valley. It was a strangely calming scene.

Bing.

Wilfred's perso-text gave the signal for an incoming message. That would be Mum. He didn't press the receive button, but started the bike and began the winding descent to the lake, past the yacht club and holiday cabins and onto the road that had barely changed in the last six months. The worst of the potholes had been filled, but the increase in traffic made the road, if anything, more dangerous than it had been before communications were opened to Willowvale. He reached the far crest of the crater and felt he was really on his way.

Willowvale had changed a lot since he last saw it. The town wall was already falling into disrepair, and houses were growing like weeds outside what had previously been the town area. Some new houses were built in an amusing parody of O'Malley fashions. Some of the ruins had been rebuilt haphazardly, but with homely charm and touches of individuality—swans made from old tyres, tree stumps carved into figures. They were very different from the austere, poverty-stricken look of six months before.

Wilfred remembered well the way to Cassie's house. He was glad that the changes here made him unnoticeable, with other motor vehicles mingling with horse drawn carts, bicycles and various eccentric conveyances made from junk and pulled by everything from goats to cars.

His knock on the door echoed inside the house. An empty, nobody-home kind of sound. Wilfred peered through a glass pane by the door but all he saw were shadows distorted by the textured, coloured glass. He knocked again. No answer. He walked round by a shady side path to the back door, but all the curtains were closed and there was no sign of anyone at home.

Wilfred sat on the back step. His perso-text binged again. Drat Mum. He was so close to being an adult. When would she back off? What should he do now? It was still hot, still light, but if he couldn't see Cassie what was the point of coming? He didn't want to go home and face Mum without the satisfaction of seeing Cassie. What should he do? Wearily he stood, feeling sweaty inside his leather jacket now that he was off the bike. He supposed there was nothing to do but go home. First, go into town and get a cool drink. Making a fool of himself as usual. He wished he could get things right, once, one day.

Down at the front gate his motorbike was surrounded by an admiring crowd of children.

"Is that yours?"

"Yes."

"Are you old enough to drive?"

"I'm older than I look." This was sadly true.

"How old are you then?"

"Very nearly sixteen."

"I don't believe you. My brother's sixteen and he looks much older than you."

"Where are you from?"

"O'Malley."

"Can we have a ride?"

"I don't have time. I have to go."

"Why were you knocking on the door?"

Did they ever stop asking questions? "I wanted to see them. But they aren't there. They're my friends."

"Is Cassie your girlfriend?" The children giggled behind their hands.

"Look, it doesn't matter. They aren't home."

The children giggled and whispered.

"If you give us a ride, we'll tell you where they are."

Wilfred had given five or six kids a ride round the block and was growing very tired of children when he remembered that Cassie's family had a shack out of town. He stopped the bike at the kerb and helped the current child off. "Got to go," he said.

"Hey, we won't tell you where they are!"

"I remembered," said Wilfred, but the faces of the kids who had missed out were so disappointed that he gave them a ride too.

"You're nice," said the last child, and hugged him.

Wilfred patted her awkwardly on the head. He was used to his little cousins, but he didn't know this child. "Well, I'd better go. Shouldn't you be home for dinner?"

"Tea, you mean!" said the kids, and scattered.

The main street was quiet now. Wilfred rode past the park and along the road inside the town wall, which had collapsed almost to the ground in places. The second gateway still had its arch topped with broken glass, but the gate was gone. There was a flower bed in the middle of the entrance and more half-built houses outside.

The road to Cassie's family shack was unsealed. A woman rode a horse along it. The horse shied as Wilfred passed. "Sorry," he said, but she didn't hear. *Now, which place was it?* He slowed to a walking pace. He hadn't actually been to the shack before, but Cassie pointed it out as they'd hurried past on that last day.

"That's our country residence," she said.

"What?" asked Wilfred, taken in by her tone.

"Just a shack where we sometimes go to get away from town," she said. "I suppose…we can go there any time we want, now."

Wilfred had looked where she pointed, but could only see a dirt path leading up the hill into the bush.

This was the place. A steep path up the hillside and a building of some sort hidden under trees. Wilfred leaned the bike on a large rock. As he approached, before he saw the house, he heard the deep barking of two large dogs.

"Magda! Wolfie! Quiet!" someone yelled.

Wilfred hoped the dogs were tied up. He called out, "Hello?"

"Who is it?" called a voice that sounded a touch exasperated. Wilfred walked up to the house, if it could be called that. It was twilight now; he saw a brick wall but nothing more of a conventional building. Wooden beams, tree branches, tiles, thatch, mud, old corrugated iron sheets and other odd materials made a small shack inside the ruins of what had once been a larger house. A woman stood in the doorway, turned to talk to someone inside. Thistle. Cassie's mother. She was looking back into the hut, saying, "I don't know. First Cassie runs off, then Pip's late home and neither of them have done a thing for tea and now someone's here. Wolfie! Magda! Shut UP."

Wilfred's heart sank. He stepped forward. "Mrs Thistle…? It's Wilfred…"

Thistle stepped back, nearly tripping.

"Cassie's friend from O'Malley, Wilfred." Then he remembered he still had his helmet on. As he took it off, Thistle's posture relaxed. Oh. Cassie had once been kidnapped—by men on motorbikes. His friends, if he could still call them that. Apologetically he held the helmet behind him. "Cassie's friend from O'Malley. I thought I'd, um, drop in and say hello."

More barks from the dogs indicated another arrival. Thistle's recovery of equilibrium and more conventional greeting were drowned. Another voice called from inside the house, "What's wrong with the dogs tonight?" and Cassie walked out of the top of the path into the open area in front of the shack.

"Wilfred!" Cassie launched herself at Wilfred and hugged him so tightly he nearly overbalanced. "I'm so glad to see you!"

It was almost dark, but as Cassie hugged him, Wilfred thought he felt tears on her cheek.

Thistle heard something in her voice. "What's wrong?"

"It's Pip. He's gone." Cassie's brother. Wilfred still thought of him as Radcliffe, the cool, slightly older member of the bike group the Gentlemen of the Road, of which Wilfred had once been the youngest member. Ivan called him Phil. A slippery character, in Wilfred's thoughts, with all those names.

CHAPTER THREE
NO ANSWERS

"What do you mean, gone?" Cassie's father came to the door.

"I mean gone back to that other place where Ivan and Reenie came from."

"How can you know that?"

"I'm telling you, he's gone."

"How could he go there? You told us that it only happened when the curfew drums were playing here, and drums playing there at the same time. At sunset. The chances of that happening since the curfew was taken away are nil."

"He's gone. I saw it with my own eyes. John was up there with the old curfew drum. They must have had some drums playing at the other end too." Cassie told them everything that had happened.

Thistle slumped against the door post as if her strength drained away with this news. "How could he?" she said quietly. Raven put his arm around her and drew her inside the shack where their voices could be heard rising and falling like the wind in trees—though Wilfred and Cassie weren't listening.

Cassie sat down on a rock and put her head in her hands. Wilfred stood uncertainly for a moment, then sat down next to her. He didn't know what to say or do. The rock was uncomfortable because Cassie was sitting in the middle, leaving little space for him. He stood up again, and fidgeted with the strap of his helmet.

"What are we going to do?" Cassie groaned.

"I don't know," said Wilfred. His perso-text binged its tune yet again. Without thinking he pressed the "accept" button and a long ribbon of coded message tape wound out of it like a small snake. He absently stuffed it in his pocket. *Why, oh why, did things always go wrong*, he thought. He could feel his mother's anger heating the paper messages, and felt that if he wasn't careful, they would ignite in his pocket; but this thought soon faded. Cassie was pleased to see him, he thought, but this drama was bigger than seeing him. Drat Cal. How could he be so selfish?

Cassie looked up when she heard the noises from Wilfred's perso-text. She shifted over so he could sit. "Sorry," she said. "I'm really, really glad to see you. But this is such a disaster."

"Why?" asked Wilfred thoughtlessly.

"He's only just come back. Everything was going well…"

Wilfred's device binged again.

"Does that thing ever stop making noises?"

"It's my mother."

"You should answer."

"I don't want to."

There was silence on Cassie's side of the rock. Wilfred felt her stiffen. "Pip went on purpose this time. He didn't want to stay here with us." Her voice was very quiet. "He wanted to be with Reenie, didn't he?" she said.

Wilfred didn't know if she expected an answer.

"We have to do something," said Cassie.

"I don't think so." Wilfred and Cassie both jumped. Thistle and Raven stood behind them in the dark.

"What do you mean?" said Cassie, the pitch of her voice rising.

"We've discussed it. He's old enough to decide for himself. He's an adult," said Thistle tiredly. "He's chosen to go."

"No!" yelled Cassie. "He can't do this! She grabbed Wilfred's wrist and stood up, dragging him to his feet too. "Maybe you don't love me either, seeing as you evidently don't care about him."

"We do care," said Raven, "of course we do."

"No you don't. I hate you both."

"Cassie. Don't—"

Cassie, still holding Wilfred's wrist, started down the dark track toward the road, skilfully negotiating rocks and bends, dragging him along, muttering, "I'll show them. I'll show them."

"Cassie!" her parents' voices floated after them, but they didn't follow. The dogs barked once, desultorily.

Cassie jumped onto the seat of the bike, making it rock dangerously on its stand. "Take me somewhere."

Many feelings churned inside Wilfred. He grabbed the handlebars. "Where?"

"We have to get him back."

"How?"

Cassie had no answer to this. "Let's just go somewhere. I can't stand it here."

Wilfred wanted to say: *Why do you care so much about your brother and nothing for me?* But he didn't. He didn't know a lot about brothers and sisters. *I came to see you. It's not fair,* were the next sentences that nearly escaped him. He held his tongue.

The motorcycle teetered on its stand as Cassie shook its handlebars. "Come on, Wilfred."

"There's nothing we can do. I might as well go home and leave you with your parents."

"Don't you understand? I don't want to be near them. Can't we go for a drive somewhere? I have to get away."

Wilfred understood that.

"We could go to your place. I'll drive if you don't want to."

Wilfred didn't think so. He shook his head.

Cassie grunted in frustration. "Let's go up to the ridge and see if we can find any clues. Maybe if I get the drum back, we can fix it up. Then there'd be a chance at least, that he could come back one day."

Wilfred was doubtful about this, but it was the best suggestion so far. Cassie didn't want to stay here, he wanted to see her, and…and, well, it wouldn't do any harm. "Okay."

The town was dark but for a few dim lights in windows and a single lamp shining in the park. Up the hill, near the old high school, the land opened to the sky. There was no moon. The headlight of Wilfred's bike lit a disc of ground ahead. Cassie directed him into narrow, neglected streets. It was a place Wilfred had not seen before. His only previous visit to this part of town had been on the occasion of that raid with the Gentlemen— an odd bikie gang if ever there was one—and, though it had led to his friendship with Cassie and Ivan, he preferred not to think about the night when they had first met.

The streets they passed through were too far from the centre of the town for many people to have moved there yet. Ruined houses one after another loomed in the periphery of Wilfred's headlight. Trees crept close to them, silent slow-motion warriors reclaiming their territory. It was the edge of the town, where streets faded into bush.

"Stop. Leave the bike here," said Cassie.

Walking carefully in darkness that was even murkier now that there was no headlight to contrast it with light, they rounded a bend. Wilfred saw a more complete house than the ruined shells around him. A lamp hanging in a tree illuminated the front wall made, similarly to Cassie's shack, from the remains of the original repaired with scrap materials, branches and anything to hand. A brick chimney stood its full height, smothered in ivy. Smoke curled from a small campfire. It looked like a house from a fairy tale.

Cassie grabbed Wilfred's hand. "Stop here."

Wilfred stopped.

"This is John's house."

"Who is John?"

"He's the leechy slimeball who helped Pip go to that other place. I need to talk to him. I'll sort him out."

Maybe I simply don't understand anyone, thought Wilfred, as he followed Cassie through an overgrown front yard toward the light. Her mess of curly hair seemed to spark with anger, like the tail of a frightened cat. He came here to see the Cassie who was his friend, who was enthusiastic and more real than anyone else he knew. But she was all anger now. All this strange, one-sided, unbalanced concern for her brother. No consideration for her parents, odd as their reaction to the situation was, or to him. Yes, he knew he was being pathetically self-centred and self-pitying. He admitted to himself that he had a crush on her. The sad thing was that the unfortunate turn of events this evening was chipping away at this long-nurtured feeling. Cassie was as beautiful as ever, but was she the person he'd imagined? He hurried to catch up with her, anger heating his thoughts.

In a clearing in front of the house was an idyllic scene. A young woman sat in a chair made from curved branches, suspended like a swing from the branch of a tree. She held a baby. Beneath the lamp Wilfred had seen from the street, a man sat at a picnic table. The small campfire burnt low in a ring of stones and the smell of food floated in the air. Cassie's angry approach was unheard by the couple, as the baby was crying loudly. Despite this, Wilfred couldn't bear the thought of the red-hot missile that was Cassie right now smashing into their contented cocoon of golden light.

As silently as possible, Wilfred threw himself across the space that separated him from Cassie. He seized her by the elbow and spun her around. The angry, aggressive Wilfred he'd cultivated when he joined the Gentlemen, that he thought was a facade long demolished, emerged from somewhere inside him. "Stop! What do you think you're doing?" he hissed.

"I'm going to…to…confront the bastard. Let me go!"

The baby's cries grew louder.

"You can't do that! Look at them." Unwillingly, Cassie looked. The man had put down his tools and he and the woman both leaned over the baby in concern. They wrapped it more securely in a rug, picked up the lamp and disappeared into the house.

"Everybody has their own reasons for doing things. I have my reasons for coming here. You have your reasons for being angry. Pip has his reasons for doing what he did." He drew Cassie back toward the street. She let him do it. Her stiff elbow loosened within Wilfred's fingers and his own anger dissolved. They walked in silence back to the motorbike. Cassie took the handlebars and turned the bike around, pushing it down the hill toward the main road. Gently, Wilfred took the handlebars from her grasp and they walked absorbed in their own thoughts through the dark streets.

Cassie sighed, and eventually said, "I guess I'm most angry with Pip for leaving me behind so soon. All my life I've admired him so much. I feel as if I've been running as fast as I can, trying to keep up with him ever since I can remember. To catch up. But I thought finding him and bringing him home last winter was the end of that. I thought I'd finally caught up. And now he's gone somewhere I'll never get to. He must really love Reenie to do what he did. It's too much. I can't go there…" Her voice faded sadly.

Wilfred was unsure what she meant. Could she never go to Reenie's world, or could she never fall in love? "It's a bit early to say that," he said in answer to both of these possible questions.

"I was SO angry with John. He helped Pip get out of here, and he was so rude to me. Maybe I'm mostly angry about that. Maybe I'm angry because he was so…so…He didn't care what I thought or what I did, or said. He didn't care." She sniffed. "I didn't tell you exactly what happened—what I saw. John was playing the drum, hitting it again and again. It was sunset. They knew what they were doing. I knocked the drum out of his hands and it fell. Smashed. Pip was gone. The drum's gone. Forever. John just… just brushed me off like an insect. He was laughing at me."

"Maybe he knew how important it was to Pip," said Wilfred without realizing that he'd spoken. "I suppose it is that important to Pip, or he would have stayed."

Cassie sniffed again.

At that moment Wilfred's perso-text binged.

"It's your mother. You should read her message."

Wilfred put the key in the bike's ignition and turned on the headlights so he could read the chain of messages that he had ignored all evening.

I'm so worried about you.

Please come home.

Come, I need you.

It's important.

I love you.

Then there was one that was incomplete: *W lfre . Pl a e come.* The message decayed into a series of random letters, as if her perso-text had been dropped or the buttons pressed by mistake. Wilfred looked at his watch. It was only nine-ish. He'd left at five. He hadn't been gone all that long. He showed the tape message to Cassie, then remembered she couldn't read the code, and read the messages to her.

"Mum's never said things like that before. That's odd. Even last year when I used to go off with the Gentlemen, she would just yell."

"You should go," said Cassie.

"I came to see you, and it's all gone wrong."

"Yes."

"I guess your parents are worried too, even if they seem so, um, re-signed to Pip leaving."

"You could stay a little while. You can tell your mother where you are, with that thing. The person-code thing."

"I guess I can." Wilfred's anger toward Berenice was faded. He entered a message. *Back by 11:00. Love W.*

Almost immediately an answer returned. *ASAP. Please.*

Wilfred and Cassie pushed the bike another block further until, with unspoken agreement, they decided they were far enough from John and Jules' house for distance to mask the noise of the engine. Soon they were back at Cassie's place. Wilfred took off his helmet while Cassie dismounted.

"Sorry," they both said at once.

"Sorry I didn't come sooner," said Wilfred.

"Sorry it's all a mess," said Cassie.

"Sorry I didn't write—" A sudden inspiration came over Wilfred. He took the perso-text out of his pocket. "Have this. I've paid for another hundred messages or so. It's easy to read. 1 is A, 2 is B, you'll work it out…"

"But—"

"Turn the handle."

"But, Wilfred, what about—"

"I can save up for another one." He shoved the helmet onto his head to hide his embarrassment. "Bye. I'll send a message to you when I get one. Just press the reply button—the yellow one—then we can…" Wilfred couldn't think of anything else to say. He tightened the strap on his helmet, and drove away.

CHAPTER FOUR
UP LATE

In almost every way, Jess liked O'Malley better than Willowvale. It was like coming home. There were shops full of clothes and cafes full of cakes, and everything was painted shiny and new. She quickly made many friends and now had the kind of social life that had only been a dream in the past. It was a shame her mother had refused to come to O'Malley. It was the first time Jess remembered her ever doing anything to oppose Daddy. All her childhood memories were of Mother standing back, always giving way to Daddy. Jess, though surprised at Mother's refusal after all the years of quiet acquiescence, wasn't particularly bothered at the time; but now, quite often, she missed her.

Anyway, that was the last thing on her mind right now. A night of fizzy, probably alcoholic drinks (you never could quite tell with the drinks here), crazy colourful sugary desserts only imagined back in Willowvale, plus loud music, lights and dancing certainly unimagined there obliterated most thoughts from her mind. She said goodbye to the boy who dropped her off at the door of the new house—a kiss that meant nothing—managed to fight his wandering hands off with a mention of Daddy and a quick-practised twist and unlocking door movement.

Jess leaned on the inside of the locked door with something like relief while her new admirer drove away disappointed. She walked unsteady down the hall to the kitchen, drank one of those delicious flavoured milk drinks that everyone had in their fridge here—everyone had a fridge—none of those old meat safes and ice cellars like they still had in Willowvale. This house was much like the one Daddy had built in Willowvale, but better because it was in O'Malley and everything in it worked. Jess left the milk carton on the bench and wove to her room. It was quite early for a Thursday, but she was tired. O'Malley school was more work than Willowvale school. Actually, she'd finished school back there. Now she had to catch up. Not that she was worried about it. She hadn't liked that boy much. *What was his name? Never mind.*

Jess switched on the light in her bedroom. A riot of colour hit her eyes. She took a step back in surprise…not because of the colours, which she had chosen herself when they moved in, but because her father was lying on her pink bedspread, his corpulent body ludicrous amongst the polka-dots, frilled pillows and crowd of disapproving soft toys. He woke with a start and said, "Oh, Jess. I've had an awful evening."

"Get off my bed," said Jess.

"That woman. Your m…" he rolled over and put his face into the pillow.

"Forget Mother. Now get out of my room." Jess pulled at his arm.

"I thought you'd understand."

Jess, who was tall and strong, managed to roll her father over and pull his unresisting bulk onto the edge of the mattress, where he teetered for a moment then fell to the carpeted floor (also superior to any in Willowvale). "I want to go to bed. Get out. You've got your own room. Use it." She pulled him to a sitting position. "Go on. Leave."

"I thought my princess would understand."

"Get out!" Jess pulled at his arm until he stumbled to his feet. "You're drunk. You've been fighting again." He had scratches down his cheek and signs of a developing black eye. She pushed him into the corridor and slammed her door. Ignoring his knocks and cries of "I thought my little girl would listen to me," which soon faded to mumbles and retreating footsteps, she undressed and had a shower in the exciting O'Malley-style ensuite bathroom.

Daddy was drunk. Again. It was boring and selfish of him. Yeah, he used to sit around with the men he called his mates back in Willowvale, with a beer at the pub or a whiskey at home, but it never affected him the way it did now. Feeling better after the shower, Jess found her father in the lounge room, where he was collapsed on the leather couch. "It's not fair. They've ruined my life," he muttered into the cushions, over and over.

"You'll feel better soon," said Jess unsympathetically, and went to bed.

It must have been an hour later. Jess was tired but unable to sleep. Images of the evening played through her mind. Lights, music, faces, all in a confusing kaleidoscopic whirl.

The phone rang. Jess waited for Daddy to answer it, but he didn't. It rang and rang. The shrill electronic sound was magnified by the hour and the emptiness of the house. Unexpectedly, Jess missed Mother. The house was emptier without her than Jess could have imagined. She ignored the phone. There were still none in Willowvale, so it can't have been Mother ringing. And who else would call in the middle of the night? She rolled over and put a pillow over her head. Through it, the muffled sound of the telephone continued for a few more rings, then stopped. Jess started to relax at last.

The phone rang again.

"Daddy!" Jess called half-heartedly. "The phone." He didn't hear her, or it. The ringing continued. "I'll never get to sleep," she thought and sat up angrily. That was a bad idea. She felt ill in the stomach, and the abrupt movement made her head spin and ache. She ran for the bathroom. Snores from the lounge indicated Daddy's continued presence there. Jess went to the kitchen, still brightly lit with the painful O'Malley electricity that she should be used to by now. The lights from the old diesel generator back home in Willowvale were dimmer, even though they were so much brighter than everyone else's candles and kerosene lamps. Jess stopped in the middle of the shiny tiled kitchen floor and felt a pang of homesickness so strong that she felt unsteady—and this time it was nothing to do with the last couple of pineapple mystery smoothies with green lime and caramel syrup.

The phone rang again.

Jess picked up the receiver and yelled into it, "Stop bothering me." She slammed it down into the phone cradle.

Immediately it rang again.

Jess picked up the receiver, ready to yell abuse at this nuisance caller, but before she could speak a male voice said, "Tell Rexy that if he ever, ever, does that to Berenice ever again, I will personally come and beat the…the…I'll beat him up so hard he won't forget it."

Jess, shocked, was silent.

"Did you hear?" said the voice.

"I heard."

"Tell him. And if he contacts her at all, I will also come 'round and deal with him. Do you understand?"

"He didn't do it. Whatever you think it is he did. Leave us alone."

"Does he have a black eye and a fake fingernail in his collar? Tell. Him." The caller hung up. Jess could almost hear him slamming the phone down.

Jess didn't want to, but she crept into the lounge room and looked closely at Daddy. His left eye showed more signs of bruising than before. The three bloody scratches down his cheek showed dark in the reflected light from the kitchen.

"Why would he have a fake fingernail?" Jess thought. "That creep was trying to scare me…" But she crept closer. One of the scratches went down his neck; and at his shirt collar, stuck between the flesh of his neck and the starched fabric, was a grubby oval of plastic painted in the pearly colours fashionable for O'Malley ladies' fingernails. Jess felt sick again. He wasn't like that. He wasn't.

Wilfred's hand shook as he hung up the phone. Berenice was in the bath with lots of bubbles and a hot chocolate with pink marshmallows. She didn't know he'd found the phone number in her appointment diary, or even that in her distress she'd mentioned a name. Rexy. Of all the stupid names.

Berenice might not know everything Wilfred was doing, but he now realized there was plenty he didn't know about her, either. He didn't know that she had a boyfriend. Not that someone who frightened her like that, tough as she was, and hurt her, could justifiably be called a friend. And judging by the size of the baby blue linen jacket left hanging on the hallstand, "boy" was equally inappropriate.

Now wasn't the time to ask questions of his mother. He was too angry to talk to anyone after coming home to find this usually tough parent brittle and crying. Not the angry, manipulative crying he knew, but whimpering like a hurt child. Her makeup was smeared and her clothes dishevelled, but worst of all she was bruised and her hands were streaked with blood.

"What happened?"

"It's okay, darling, it's his blood," she blubbered.

"Whose? Were you mugged?"

"No, no," answered Berenice, and covered her face. One of the impressive fake nails she was so proud of was missing.

"I'm going to call the police."

"No, don't. I'm all right. Please don't. I'm fine. Go to bed. I'll be fine soon."

It was after this exchange that Wilfred thought of looking through Berenice's Filofax. She'd said it wasn't a random assault. She'd sent those disturbingly distressed messages…she'd asked him to come home. So it must have been someone she knew, someone she'd invited to the house.

Wilfred, still shaking with anger at the thought that somebody could hurt and frighten his mother so badly that she was still distressed two hours later, found her addresses and phone and perso-text numbers and codes. He flicked through the files. Name after name of people he knew, or people he knew his mother worked with. He didn't know any Rexy. Stupid name. The alphabetical section yielded nothing. In the appointments section, however, on today's date, Wilfred found a cryptic note *RB 6:00 my place (Wilfred????)* with no contact details. Working his way back he found many appointments with RB, and on a page of notes at the beginning of the diary the name Rex, and a telephone number.

The person who eventually answered sounded as unpleasant as Wilfred imagined Rex was. Some relation. Sounded young and grumpy. Wilfred did his best tough guy act to scare her. As far as he was concerned, it was important to warn this Rex off. And right now Wilfred was angry enough to go round to wherever their place was and beat up this coward, even if he was twice Wilfred's size.

Jess lay on her bed, and again a dizzying series of images, thoughts and memories flashed through her mind. Her evening out seemed pretty and innocent, where earlier it had seemed daring and edgy. "Liar!" she said out loud to the anonymous caller, but she couldn't stop thinking of the marks on her father's cheek. Even without the horrifying bloody fake fingernail, it was impossible to imagine the scratches were the result of anything but an attempt at self defence by a woman—or, she thought briefly and dismissed as ludicrous, a man with fake fingernails.

"He's not like that," she said to a teddy bear that sat on her bed. The teddy did not answer any more than the anonymous and disturbing caller answered her accusation; the caller, who, Jess thought bitterly, was probably sleeping peacefully now. She threw the teddy across the room. It bounced off the dressing-table mirror and landed with a crash amongst her perfume bottles and trinkets. "He isn't," she said, but less certainly. The headlights of a passing car entered a chink between the curtains and moved across the room.

Jess turned over. The glassy eyes of the teddy flashed knowingly. She was the liar. Daddy was like that. He was a bully. Everyone in Willowvale thought it, even his "mates". He never pushed too hard with Jess—she was well aware of her spoilt, only-child status, and the protective nature of her own volatile temper. Now pictures of Mother, who she was unaccountably starting to miss badly, came into her mind…and Mother's string of complaints; headaches, sprains, bruises— "I walked into the door in the dark, aren't I silly?"— and occasional illogical clothing: long sleeves and scarves high on her neck in summer, and her habit of wearing too much makeup, like a mask. Jess lay very still for a while. When her ashamed, scared heartbeat slowed and her breathing less resembled a crowd of toads trying to escape her lungs, she got up, fetched the teddy, and curled herself around it.

CHAPTER FIVE
EXPLORING

Ivan hurried away from the ridge. His heart beat fast and his hands were shaking as if he was scared, or angry. He thought he felt neither of these emotions, but the shock of seeing Phil appear was considerable. Yes, he and Reenie had hunted Hugo out and persuaded him to play his drums at sunset. But Ivan realized now that the last thing he expected was to actually succeed. What would happen now? He wondered what Mum and Dad would say and how Reenie would explain the situation to them.

Reenie was going to leave soon to university in O'Malley. She'd been living in university accommodation. Phil would stick around here and there like a smell. Okay. Ivan admitted it. He still had a big problem with Phil. And he wished it was Cassie who had appeared on the ridge. Or he who had gone. A few other things as well. He picked up a stone the size of a cricket ball and threw it as hard as he could into the bush. It hit a tree with a satisfying crack.

"I'm home," Ivan announced as he came in. Mum, Dad and Anna were all occupied in their usual evening activities; washing up, reading, watching television.

"You missed dinner. Again. It's on the bench."

Ivan took his plate to the table and ate, starting with potatoes, the least desirable food when cold, and working his way in a logical progression to the salad, which was cold anyway. Every moment he expected Reenie, with Phil in tow, to appear with the exciting news.

"Is Reenie coming home soon?" asked Mum. "You two usually come back together."

"No idea," said Ivan. He took his plate to the sink, and went out the back to sit with Frankie. He still felt shaky and disturbed, and Frankie's unquestioning presence would be calming. The dog had suddenly begun to show her age. The fur on her muzzle was going white, and this hot weather made her droopy. Ivan sat on the back step stroking her ears and remembering how tired he'd felt before the adventure began last year. The tiredness of things going badly. The adventure that took him and Reenie to the place that was identical to and yet completely different from here. He'd thought that the weary, colourless Ivan who found everything difficult of a few months ago was gone; but perhaps tonight's events threatened to bring that Ivan back.

"She's got a lot to do," Dad said to Mum. "When is she going to get her act together?"

"At least Anna is still a civilized age," said Mum, thinking Ivan was out of earshot. He snorted. Mum should know that girls Anna's age were more poisonous than everyone else put together. He thought of the impending situation with a lovestruck Reenie and Phil forcibly inserted into everyone's life. It was not a pretty thought. Frankie, discerning some of Ivan's unhappiness, turned her head and gazed sympathetically into his eyes.

"Everything is going wrong. Can you feel it? Some days are like that, some weeks, even some months. This is just the beginning," Ivan said to Frankie. He couldn't stand the situation, even though it had not fully taken hold yet. He had to get away. Now, or as soon as possible. Leaving Frankie sitting on the step, he went to his room, tipped everything from his school backpack out onto the floor and packed. A shirt. A jacket. His phone. He took a piece of paper from a school notebook and wrote. *Dear Mum and Dad, I am going to explore the bush above Leo's place. I've got food and water. And everything. Back Sunday night (probably). Love, Ivan.* He folded the note and put it into an old envelope that was lying on his desk. On the outside of the envelope he wrote another message: *Left early. Ivan.* There. If he was lucky they would be happy with that part of the message and not find the rest of it until the evening. School might be a problem. They'd notice he was absent. Oh well. He could sort it out on Monday.

School started a fortnight or so ago. His second-last year. There were things to be said both in favour and against school. Ivan liked it more this year than he admitted out loud—in some ways. But the constant insistence on how important this year was, and how difficult it would be and how much work…well, even if nobody put it in exactly those words, that was the message he perceived. He needed a day off. He could catch up.

The straps of the backpack bit into Ivan's shoulders. He reviewed its contents in his mind. Water. Some food that he'd picked up on his way out of the house this morning. Matches. A small tarpaulin. A jacket, spare shirt and a knife. Should he have brought a compass? No, he knew this area well. Ivan shifted the backpack to a more comfortable position. It wasn't very heavy, no heavier than when he had his school things in it. He felt in his pocket for his phone. His parents would probably ring this afternoon. He was too old for them to constantly worry, but they were still traumatized by his and Reenie's disappearance last winter, and their lack of an explanation of what had happened or where they had been. Mum and Dad didn't know that this was not actually a refusal, but in fact their inability to explain. They tried to tell their parents that everything was simply too complicated, but they didn't understand. Well, when they found his note they would know everything about this trip. Where? Going up the bush behind Leo's place, the next ridge over from the one behind their own house. How long? Back before Monday. He imagined the conversation: *"But why are you doing this?"* "I want to go out in the bush and survive." He imagined his parents' glance at each other, and he saw the thought pass between them—*let him go, he needs the space*—or whatever it is parents think when they decide not to stop you from doing something that they don't really want you to do.

He came to the bottom of the gully that led down from the power poles to the more open valley. The track crossed a disused paddock that was now a reserve. He walked out of the shadow of the first ridge and felt the sun on the back of his head. The day was going to be hot. Ivan wished he'd brought a hat. He reached the road with its line of trees and welcomed the shade. Forested hills rose in front of him. There was a fence, but it looked as if no-one had been past it for years, or used the land for anything at all.

I want to be by myself, Ivan thought. School was claustrophobic, but the situation with Reenie and Phil, and the complications that would produce, was going to be much worse. He found a gate, locked, and looked round to check that nobody was watching. Then feeling stupidly surreptitious, he climbed over it and entered the forest.

It was beautiful. Only a couple of kilometres from the centre of town, and yet completely unspoiled. He climbed up a creek bed that rose gently into the hills, full of sculptured boulders with clefts holding secretive pools of black water. Sandy bends were decorated with the tracks of wombats and wallabies. Avoiding any direction that would lead to civilization, Ivan adjusted his backpack straps again and continued with no other aim than to temporarily lose himself.

As he walked, Ivan felt the beauty of the landscape sink down over him like mist, calming the agitation that had stirred him since Phil's arrival. Not that he'd been involved in the long, serious and tense conversation that occurred between Reenie and their parents with Phil. He had been an unwilling spectator, subject, and sometimes participant, last night. Ivan stayed in his room. After a short time, Anna had come in, hugging Frankie to her chest, upset.

"What's going on? Why are they talking for so long? I want to go to bed. I need them to kiss me good night."

"Reenie found Phil again. She wants to keep him."

"What do you mean? He's not a dog."

"I don't know. I was trying to be funny."

"Well, you weren't. Can I stay with you?"

"Yeah, if you want to."

Anna curled up on Ivan's bed with a book from his shelf that he'd liked a lot at her age, Frankie at her feet. Ivan sat at his desk and tried to study. Voices from the other room bounced off the closed door. He and Anna were in a cocoon, isolated from whatever problems the others were wrestling with.

Now the silent eucalyptus trees and the morning activity of birds draped their comfort over Ivan as he climbed into the hills. He felt as if he was in a bubble, protected from the entanglements of the world. Ascending to a point where the creek fell from a flatter bowl-shaped area, he skirted this more open space and headed up one of the surrounding hills, following a well-defined foot track.

Soon, Ivan realized that this trail was not made by humans. "The only people who've been here lately are wallabies," he thought, as he ducked for the fifth or sixth time stooping under a branch too low for anyone but animals to easily pass. However, this was as good a route as any. Ivan followed it until it petered out, then found another, and another. In this fashion he travelled for some time. The sun climbed quickly up the eastern sky. Birds retreated to the secret places where birds go in the middle of the day. The only sign he saw of wallabies and kangaroos were their tracks and droppings, their campsites under shady trees, and tail marks across sandy ground. He stopped at the top of a long ridge. Trees surrounded him, obscuring the view. There was a glimpse of farmland to one side, a blue smudge of hills in the distance. The ridge dropped away down a rocky slope. Maybe he was near the river. He was thirsty and his bottle of water was nearly empty. The mysterious black pools of that first creek contained the only water he'd seen, and a person would need to be desperate to drink that. Ivan scrambled down from the hilltop, over boulder after boulder, getting tangled in bushes and scratched by twigs. The day was not turning out to be as enjoyable as he had expected; but still, something about the place calmed him.

He reached the river at an unfamiliar place, upstream of the long pool where people went to swim and paddle canoes. He swam in a rocky-bottomed pool, filled his water bottle, and himself, and considered what to do next. It was tempting to follow the river downstream to the bridge and go home. Occasionally he heard the distant sound of an engine as a vehicle climbed the steep hills that enclosed the river. It would only take half the time or less than he'd used to get here to walk home. Then he could have a cool drink without kangaroo droppings in it, a shower, and relax.

No. Reenie and her complications would still be whirling the family into emotional chaos.

Ivan packed up his things, waded across the river at a small set of rapids and, after pausing to put his boots on, started up the steep side of the river valley. The sun hung high in the sky for so long that Ivan imagined it being stuck, and time never moving from that moment. He saw a scaly tail flick into the undergrowth and at once every crooked stick on the ground was a snake.

"What am I doing?" Sweaty, sunburnt and developing blisters on his heels, Ivan sat down on a rock to rest. He drew on the ground with a stick and conducted an argument with himself.

Are you running away?

I don't know.

Yes you are. Why?

Because I don't like it.

Don't like what?

I don't know.

Why don't you like this thing you don't know?

I don't know.

You're lying.

Ivan drew a long arc in the dusty ground. *I'm jealous of Reenie. She's got Phil and I haven't got anyone. I want to see Cassie and find out if she misses me.*

So what are you going to do about it?

"I can't do anything about it, you idiot," said Ivan out loud to himself. "It's nearly impossible that anyone will ever go one way or the other to her world again."

Nearly isn't completely, said his interrogatory self. What do you want?

I want to see Cassie again. And Wilfred.

Look for another way.

But how? Ivan threw the stick down, picked up his backpack and continued pushing his way up the hill, through flowering cassinia bushes that dropped pollen and petals on his shoulders as if in encouragement.

CHAPTER SIX

INFORMATION

Cassie was still churned up. Although she had calmed outwardly, she didn't understand why Raven and Thistle were so sanguine about what she thought of as Pip's desertion. She supposed they thought of it in their heartless rational way as nothing more than a departure. Wilfred's tactless, angry question, why did she care so much more about Pip than about other people, played on her mind too. Did she really? It must seem so to Wilfred, or he would not have blurted it out. Her reply had the honesty of surprise: she had always admired Pip, looked up to him, loved him and wanted to be like him.

Now, she couldn't. Couldn't what? Couldn't be like Pip, couldn't follow him where he had gone? Or couldn't love him above everyone else any more? He was gone, he'd left her behind; he wanted to be with someone else more than with the family. With her. She was angry and sad. Still, she had to admit painfully to herself, now was the time to move on. To grow up.

That's all very well, she told herself, but Pip's still my brother. And even though we're in modern times, it's worse than the olden days when people left on sailing ships for the other side of the world. Even then they could write to each other; it might have taken a year to get a reply…but there was still the possibility of one. This was worse. He was in that other place where Ivan and Reenie came from, which might as well be another planet. She sighed and moved her school satchel full of books for Friday lessons to a better position on her shoulder.

The land was dry, though the market gardens outside the old town walls were green with lettuces and beans hand-watered from the creek. It was early. Cassie had left the shack without saying goodbye, a little ashamed of her outburst of the night before, but unwilling to apologize. It was her chore to feed the chooks and water the vegetables in the house in town. She could stay in town for a few days, and work things out, work out what she felt, what she wanted…that was a good idea. Raven and Thistle would know where she was. It was only a twenty-minute walk if they weren't sure. Let them find her.

The family's usual house in town, their main house, was more substantial than the shack. It was built of old red brick and had glass windows, three bedrooms, and even a bathroom with water piped from a tank that collected rainwater from the roof. Not like the shack where she had to constantly go and fetch water from the creek and carry the heavy buckets back up the steep hill. There was no sewerage system, just like the old days before the Disaster. The family moved freely between these two places now. Cassie suspected that her parents preferred the shack, where their workshop was located; but she loved the old house with its cool rooms, cold in winter, but with a big kitchen fireplace that heated the house, and its garden full of fruit trees. Her parents had made the garden beautiful, even while it was functional, with flowers (which had been riskily frivolous before the political upheaval of last year), a pond, and a swing that she still liked to use. It was a good place to think.

There was plenty of time to feed the hens and water the garden. Her route led past the school, which was near the centre of town, and she'd have to cut back later. Lessons weren't held in the old high school from before the Disaster, where previously illicit out-of-town dances were held, now fully legitimate and hugely popular. The older central school had old brick and weatherboard classrooms, a granite principal's house and a hall whose windows were so overgrown with ivy that it was filled with green light, like river water.

Cassie approached old Mr and Mrs Williams' house. Their son Mick was a friend of Thistle and Raven's, and bizarrely, in Ivan's world, was Ivan and Reenie's father, and old Mr and Mrs Williams were their grandparents; and Mick in their world wasn't married to Penny, but to a completely different person, who was Ivan and Reenie's mother—and it was all too mind-boggling to contemplate.

Mick and Penny Williams were there with old Mr and Mrs Williams now, taking down the last pieces of a high paling fence that had enclosed the front yard when prying eyes were a problem, until the rebellion in town last year and the departure of the town president in disgrace; when suddenly all the pointless rules dissolved into nothingness and everything started to look up.

Until Pip left.

"Good morning, young Cassie," said Mick Williams as she approached. "You don't look as happy as this fine morning should make you."

"Good morning," said Cassie.

"You look as if the weight of the world is on your shoulders," said old Mrs Williams.

Cassie felt her throat tighten. Could she answer without revealing just how much weight she felt pressing down on her?

"Is something wrong, Cassie?" asked Penny Williams.

"It's Pip," said Cassie abruptly.

"Is he sick? An accident?"

"No. He's gone. Away. Again."

"Well, he's grown up now," said old Mr Williams.

"But he's gone to Reenie. He's never coming back, he can't now, he's gone to their world," gasped Cassie, and hurried away.

Her eyes blurred, Cassie strode up the street and around the corner. She arrived at her own house and closed the gate in the high front hedge with relief. This feeling of upset and wrongness and disturbance was not showing any signs of dispersing the way she hoped. She went to the feed bin and filled the measuring can with seed for the hens.

There was a knock at the wooden gate. "Cassie? Can I come in?"

"Who is it?"

"Penny Williams."

Puzzled, Cassie opened the gate. Mrs Penny Williams was a friend of her parents, but Cassie did not know her very well, and had never spoken to her as an individual before. Penny Williams was a slim woman with neat light brown hair and fair rosy cheeks, one of those people Cassie thought always knew how to do things right. Mick was laconic and casual, Penny always seemed correct and cautious. Cassie could not understand her friendship with Thistle, who was as prickly and uncompromising as her name suggested, and rebellious (for a mother).

"I need to talk to you," said Penny as she came into the garden.

"What about?"

"I know you're very upset about your brother…what I want to talk to you about is a bit odd…you might think it silly…"

Cassie had never thought Penny, or Mrs Williams as she was accustomed to call her, as odd, eccentric or silly. On the contrary, Penny was a neatly organized person to whom those words never applied even remotely in Cassie's mind. Her participation in a number of the clandestine dances in the old high school hall was the silliest thing Cassie had ever seen her do; but that was a small act of rebellion in which many townspeople had indulged before things came to a head—of which Penny's almost-arrest had been a symptom… "Oh?" said Cassie noncommittally.

"Can we sit down? I know you have to feed the chooks and get to school, but this is complicated."

"It's okay. I don't mind being late." Cassie led the way to a bench near the fish pond.

"I don't really know where to start. The story goes back a long time. I'm guessing you are worried that you'll never see you brother—"

"Pip,"

"—again. He's gone to that other world where those two friends of yours came from?"

"Yes. He went last night."

"And you are worried that he can never come back?"

"How much do you know about that world?"

"Mick told me everything that happened. Of course he did. The boy was so sure Mick was his father, and it's true he looked uncannily like Mick at the same age. I'm not stupid, but still, it's impossible that the boy is Mick's child in this world; yet he looks just like him. Everyone would have known about it for years if Mick had a child with another woman after he was married to me. He's not like that. I trust him. Mick told me that the kids said they came from another…world, I suppose, like you say. One that they insisted was almost identical to this world, but different as well…with some of the same people in it. Mick, his parents, even me—in this other world. No wonder the boy was so confused." Her voice slowed and stopped.

Cassie coughed to remind her to continue.

"And it made me think. The boy…"

"Ivan."

"…said there had been no Disaster in his world. And I wondered if that's significant. Then I remembered. Your parents came to Willowvale not long after the Disaster. I've been wondering what happened to them, getting here. We were very isolated for a long, long time when it happened. Stirling and Walagu were destroyed; we were lucky to be spared. The roads were cut. Every tree from Stirling to Walagu and further knocked flat. Stock killed, people dead. Complete destruction. We were all traumatized. You weren't born; you wouldn't know, but it really was indeed a terrible disaster. I'm not exaggerating. And Raven and Thistle appeared, out of the forest like characters from a fairy tale. They were pretty knocked about, filthy, grazed, skinny; and had nothing but backpacks and the clothes they stood up in. There was no way of getting in or out from here for months, years. And they stayed. They were young, not more than teenagers, maybe Pip's age…"

"They've never said anything about it to me."

"They looked pretty shell-shocked when they came. It's difficult to remember. It was a hard time for all of us, and we maybe didn't pay as much attention as we should. We didn't ask, and I dare say they don't want to talk about it. I was only a teenager too, I didn't think much about it."

Cassie was silent. Sun glinted off the pond, and the fowls crowded to the wire, clucking for their meal.

Penny looked at her for a long moment, then said, "I think they came from that other place. You should ask them how they came; because you might be able to get to that place again somehow. Mick told me about the way Ivan and his sister came and Pip went, the curfew drums and the sunset thing. I think that was a lucky coincidence. I think there's another way between these two worlds. Raven and Thistle might know the way."

Cassie's heart beat fast. "You really think so? Why? Couldn't Thistle and Raven have come from somewhere in the real—the proper—this—world, and got lost here?"

"Well… I suppose it's possible. But they seemed so different, so puzzled. And they've never really fit in, not that that bothers me…but…I guess I always vaguely felt that they were from a different world, in some odd way. They don't have any relations, or talk about any. I don't know. There was always something unexpected about them, and they always seemed to find things so unexpected, too. Now I think maybe they actually came through from that other world somehow. You should ask them. Perhaps you can see your brother again, if they still know, if it's true, if…"

her voice trailed away again.

"They've never said anything. Not a word. They've never tried to go anywhere."

"Maybe they like it here. Or liked it at first, or didn't know what was happening. Then Pip was born. It could be that it was too difficult to return that way with a baby. Two babies…"

Cassie could barely stay still. She couldn't. She jumped up. "I'll talk to them. Thanks, Mrs Williams."

"Call me Penny."

There was no point going to school. Cassie quickly fed the hens and watered the vegetables, and hurried back to the shack by a circuitous route, hoping not to meet too many other students, or worse, teachers, and have to explain what she was up to. Not that she cared. This was too important.

Raven and Thistle looked uncomfortable as they and Cassie sat down in the shade outside the shack. Cassie felt anxious too. It had been difficult enough to persuade them to leave their work, which they loved; and the words "talk about something important" are always alarming one way or another.

When Cassie explained her conversation with Penny, her parents looked puzzled, then surprised and alarmed.

"Excuse us for a moment." said Raven, and they stood and disappeared into the shack, closing the door firmly behind them and even lowering the bolt from the inside before Cassie could object. Cassie, completely mystified, knocked. "Come back in half an hour. We need to discuss this. We'll talk to you then. We promise." Cassie took the dogs and walked to the ridge above the house, an old cleared area from where the town could be seen settled into its valley-bowl like an animated map. She sat down in the shade of a wattle tree, not knowing what to think about any of the odd occurrences of the last couple of days: of Pip's lovestruck departure, of her parents' odd behaviour, of Wilfred's mysterious and unexpected visit. Wilfred. The perso-text. He might send a message soon. Dear Wilfred—oops, she sounded like Mrs Williams (the older), Ivan's grandmother. Cassie had never had a grandmother, grandfather, or any relations. She stood up, stretched, whistled for the dogs, and returned to the shack to interview her parents.

"So. I need you to tell me how you came here. Maybe I can go and find Pip, or he can come back one day."

"You do understand that Pip is an adult—or as close to one as can be—reckless and inexperienced though he is," said Raven.

"Don't you care about him? About what could happen to him?"

"Of course we care! We're heartbroken," said Thistle.

"He's chosen to go," said Raven.

"He chose the other time too, and you did everything you could to find him. I don't understand."

Raven sighed and put his hand on Thistle's knee. They looked at each other as if to gain strength, or wisdom. "Very well. We'll tell you. But use this trust wisely. Everything we do in life has its consequences, and not all consequences are good."

"We asked you to give us time just now because what Penny told you, her theory, is something we have suspected, wondered about, for a long time."

"Have you talked to her about it?"

"It's not easy, it has never been easy or even possible to talk to people here about anything," said Thistle.

"But what happened? How did you come to be here? Is what Mrs Williams said likely to be true? Haven't you ever wondered about it, or tried to find out?"

"Calm down, Cassie."

"How can I calm down? How can you two be so cold about it?"

"You're worrying the dogs. Please calm yourself and we'll tell you. Perhaps we should have told you and Pip long ago."

Cassie looked at the dogs. Both Wolfie and Magda watched her with anxious brown eyes. She took a deep breath and patted her thigh for them to come closer. She stroked their wiry fur until she felt more under control. "Please tell me."

CHAPTER SEVEN
RESTLESSNESS

Thistle and Raven sat silently. The dogs watched them nervously, sensing their discomfort.

Cassie thumped her knee in frustration. "You have to talk if you're going to tell me anything."

"We're not used to talking, we're used to holding our tongues," said Thistle, and shut her mouth with a snap.

"It was a long time ago. Like Thistle said, we're not good at talking. You ask questions, Cassie, and we'll try to answer them," said Raven. "We want you to know, but it's difficult for us, too. We aren't sure, ourselves, about a lot of things."

Cassie sighed. Thistle looked like a school kid who had been sent to the principal and didn't know why she was in trouble. Behind his beard, Raven looked apprehensive too. She felt as if she was the adult and they were the teenagers. It was an amusing thought.

"Start at the beginning," prompted Raven. "Ask us. It will make it easier. You know we're no good at telling stories, Cassie."

"Okay." Cassie sat straight up with her hands on her knees. The beginning. What was the beginning? She remembered her passing envy of Ivan, because he had grandparents, while she did not; but everybody has grandparents, somewhere. Neither of her parents had ever mentioned their family to her. "Where did you come from? Do I have grandparents?" was a good a question to start with.

"I came from Walagu. My parents worked in O'Malley. They drove there every day in the car," said Raven. "It was called commuting. Lots of people did it."

"My parents had a farm in the hills over the river, near there. Between Walagu and Stirling."

"So your parents—my grandparents—are all dead?" It wasn't really a question. Cassie knew perfectly well that the two towns mentioned had been lost in the Disaster. Walagu was completely obliterated; in its place was the large crater that had filled with water from the nearby river, its course altered. Stirling was demolished by the blast of the Disaster but still in place, a dismal monument of flattened buildings and fallen trees. She'd seen both places. Her parents looked down. She heard their joint intake of breath and suddenly saw them feeling as she'd feel if she went from one day having both mother and father, to having none. The jolt of realization physically shook her. A moment ago, seeing her parents as teenagers had been amusing. Now it was painful. With an effort she shut this feeling away, along with the many questions about these lost relations that came into her mind. "How did you get here? What happened? Why did you leave home?"

"It was a restless time. There was something in the air. I went walking in the hills behind the farm. To tell the truth I was angry. Some argument with my mother. I forget what it was about. These things that seem so important…I slammed out of the house with my backpack and a few things, to get some time alone, to sort myself out," said Thistle. "Then I got lost."

"Lost?" Cassie found it difficult to imagine Thistle lost. She had an uncannily good sense of direction. "How old were you?" The situation Thistle described reminded Cassie of something she would do herself, or would like to do.

"I was sixteen."

"Sixteen?" Cassie did a quick calculation in her head. Yes. That added up with the time of the Disaster and Thistle's age now. Sixteen. The same age as Cassie.

"Something similar happened to me. I was exploring the hills across the river from Walagu with some friends. Wild hills we'd looked at all our lives and never visited," said Raven.

"Did you get lost too?"

"Not exactly. I always knew approximately where I was; at least in a general sense," said Raven defensively.

"How did you end up here?"

"It wasn't as simple as you seem to think. Be patient, Cassie."

"I was so angry I walked and walked, not knowing what I was doing, where I was going," Thistle continued. "Over the first range of hills, then down, and up. It got dark. I was scared then, when I realized I was lost. I camped behind a fallen tree, lying in the dead leaves."

"Raven? Were you angry too? And…you weren't together?"

"We didn't even know each other. Thistle studied correspondence school and I went to school in O'Malley."

Cassie paused to absorb this information, and said nothing.

"I wasn't angry," Raven continued. "I became separated from my friends, I don't know how. It was rough country, very rough. Steep gullies, confusing ridges, and thick forest. I yelled and yelled, looked for them. They were nowhere. Luckily I had a tarpaulin and a few things; food, matches…"

"What happened? When did you two meet? How?"

"I lost track of how long I was out there. About three days, maybe. I suppose I should have stayed in one place. It would have been easier for them to find me. That's what people tell you to do when you're lost, but in practise it's extremely difficult."

Thistle broke in. "We were wandering around separately. We didn't know the other one was there, we didn't even know that the other existed. I was getting desperate. I only had enough food for one day, and of course I'd eaten most of it before I realized I was lost."

"Luckily I was carrying some of the group's food. We shared the weight out among us, and I had some of the camping gear too. Not everything, but enough."

"Well, I hadn't eaten for a whole day, or more. I had no idea where I was or, if I was walking toward home or away from it. I was sunburnt, scratched, exhausted, thirsty, scared. I lost track of time", said Thistle.

"Why didn't you at least know which way was north?" asked Cassie.

"I was young. I have changed a lot since then. I've learnt a lot. You can't imagine how much I've changed."

"I felt the same way as Thistle did out there. I was only young. My friends and I had gone out there for a bit of fun and it wasn't fun any more. I was scared stiff, even if I would never have admitted it."

"It was late in the day. I knew it would be dark soon, and by then I was more scared of falling down a cliff than of being hungry," said Thistle. "I found a creek bed with a few pools of water deep between rocks. I had a drink—by now I didn't care about mosquito wrigglers or rotten leaves or anything. I had forgotten to bring any matches, so I couldn't light a fire for company or for light, so I headed uphill to get closer to the sky. Even if there was no moon, I'd see the stars and feel the difference between the land and the sky. I found that comforting. The gully felt claustrophobic in the dark."

Cassie had never heard her mother make such a long speech. She felt Raven move restlessly beside her. The story was pouring out of both of them, changing the way she saw them; transforming them from reserved, wise, inscrutable parents to scared teenagers. It was weird. "So how did you meet up out there? Did you meet then? How did you end up in Willow-vale?"

Raven said, "I had a good campsite that night, in a small open area near the top of a ridge. I set up a shelter with the groundsheet I had, and lit a fire to cook some dried peas, which were about the only food I had left. There was a trickle of water coming out of a tiny soak above—not quite big enough to call it a creek. The birds were making their evening sounds and although the sun had set, it wasn't dark yet. I heated some water in the billy…the fire made the darkness thicken around me, so all I could see were the flames, and if I looked up, the sky through the trees."

"I was still a long way off when I smelt the smoke. I thought there was a bushfire. I couldn't let myself hope that it was another person. I headed toward it, not knowing what I'd do when I found the fire, wondering what I would do if it *was* a bushfire, hoping against logic that it was another person," said Thistle.

"I watched the water, waiting to cook the peas. It was getting quite dark. I heard noises…twigs breaking…rustling leaves. At first I thought it as a wombat or a kangaroo. Then I worried it might be a wild dog or pig. Then my imagination took over and gave me escaped criminals, serial killers, ghosts… I stood up and held a big stick in front of me like a sword. I could see the flames of my fire and shadowy darkness. I lost sight of anything else but the flames and the dark, and my fear.

"I walked for a long time through the bush before I actually saw the fire."

"I stood there like an idiot, too scared to relax my guard, for what seemed like an hour, but was probably only a few minutes. The noises in the bush came closer…"

"I saw that it was a small campfire, shining there like a friendly light. It wasn't a bushfire. I knew there would be a person. I could hardly believe my luck."

"I was ready for whatever was coming, except—"

"I pushed past the last line of trees and saw the campfire and a figure."

"Maybe in the back of my mind I hoped it was somebody looking for me. Then I saw that it was a girl. I can't say I was pleased, or disappointed. I simply couldn't believe my eyes."

The hair on the back of Cassie's neck was standing up. "Was that the first time you met?"

"Yes."

"But you lived near each other. How could you not know each other already?"

"Our paths hadn't crossed. We told you. I did correspondence school, and Raven went to school in O'Malley."

"I thought she was some kind of ghost," said Raven, going on with the story.

"So," said Cassie, "how did you end up at Willowvale?"

"It was a long time before we got to Willowvale," said Thistle, in a tone that implied that the question was foolish.

Cassie was relieved in an odd way to see a flash of the normal, abrupt Thistle. She felt as if she'd pushed the boulder of her parents' story off the mountaintop of their reserve of silence, and there was nothing that would stop it from taking its own course until it reached the end of its journey at the very bottom of the mountain.

"It's 'round here that the story starts to get strange," said Raven.

Cassie wasn't so sure about that. The story was already weird. She had a multitude of questions to ask and logical curiosity to be satisfied. But as far as her parents were concerned, questions were distractions.

"To cut a long story short," said Raven (Cassie doubted this), "we met. We were happy to have company in our predicament, even if neither of us knew where we were. I didn't mind sharing my food with Thistle because, well, it was so wonderful to meet another person out there…"

"…and I thought the dried peas were the best food I'd ever tasted."

"We decided to institute a methodical plan in the morning. While we were sitting there talking about it, Thistle looked up at the sky."

"I saw a planet, or a star that was brighter than any I had ever seen."

"We watched it for a while, but neither of us knew enough about astronomy to make anything of it. We thought in the end it was a planet we hadn't noticed before."

"The next morning we decided to continue along the ridge near the campsite. It was more open there. If someone sent out a small plane or a helicopter, they could see us."

"What's a helicopter?" asked Cassie.

"You've heard of aeroplanes, you know, machines like trucks or cars, but they can fly? A helicopter flies, but not in a straight line like planes; more like a dragonfly; up, down, hovering in one place. They used to use them for searches and rescuing people from difficult terrain, before the Disaster."

Cassie was not much wiser after the explanation.

"We think we travelled south. That was our guess. It was a hot day, very bright, but hazy, and it was difficult to see where the light was coming from…We were becoming dehydrated, very thirsty. A bit confused. So, when we saw it we couldn't be sure…"

"Saw what?"

"A building."

"The building existing wasn't the surprise—but it was a strange building."

Ivan was getting more and more disoriented. Something he'd eaten, or more likely some of the water from one of those dank pools, had disagreed with his stomach. He slept for a while and woke with no idea where he was or what time, or even day, it was. The illness made him feel dizzy and sick. He knew he'd wandered but had no coherent recollection of how or where. Vague memories of open fields and the disinterested stares of cows from the darkness, of climbing through barbed wire fences (he had the scratches), crossing a deserted dirt road. He had a confused, nightmare-like memory of a dry electric storm too…of lightning flashing in clouds, but no rain. His backpack, despite being empty of food and water, felt hot and heavy on his back. His head ached. He'd thrown up more generously than seemed possible. All he could see was the crowd of trees that leaned out of the hillside as if watching his passage below them…eucalypts with loosening bark, cypresses too neat to belong here, and yet they did. The cypress pines reminded him of Phil, who was named after them. Ivan had uncovered this, his real name, in a weird subconscious-knowledge coincidence. Callitris, the scientific name for cypress pine. An odd name. Ivan would rather think of Cassie, also named after a plant, Cassinia. He thought it a pretty name. There were plenty of cassinias around too: leggy, woody plants as tall as a person with shaggy, narrow drooping leaves, and bunches of pungent cream blossoms. Ivan thought of Cassie and Cal as he pushed up the ridge, clambering over boulders and fallen trees.

He saw the sky through the treetops at the lip of the ridge. It wasn't as clear as it had been when he started out yesterday—or was it the day before? The sky was a dirty colour, not the clear blue of summer. He wiped his hand across his eyes to clear them and wished he had some water. It was time to go home. When he reached the top of the ridge he'd get his bearing, head for the road (it must be nearby) and hitchhike home, or walk. When he found mobile coverage he could ring home and get them to pick him up if necessary.

It was not far to the top of the ridge. Ivan pushed on doggedly, hoping the road would be easy to see and not too far away. At last he reached the summit and surveyed the surrounding landscape through columns of tree trunks. All he could see were ranks of wooded hills rolling away like gigantic waves. Thunder clouds hung on the peaks of the farthest hills. The sky was still and hazy. A thin trail of smoke rose from a valley halfway to the horizon.

"People!" Ivan thought; but the smoke came from a valley that was steep and wild. "Oh. No. A bushfire?" For all the illness and disorientation Ivan had experienced, this was his first twinge of fear. A breeze stirred leaves above him, rattling them drily. "I've got to tell someone." He took out his phone. The battery was nearly dead and there was no signal anyway. Paying more attention to his surroundings, Ivan saw a curious cleared area at the top of a nearby hill. Straining his eyes he thought he could see a shed or house there, a small, oddly shaped, domed building. With renewed energy he hurried toward it.

"As we got nearer, the building looked stranger," said Thistle. "It wasn't a farm shed or a house. It had a dome on top, with a slit in it, an observatory."

"We were disappointed. It looked deserted."

"We went to the door and knocked anyway."

"A woman came out. She had long grey hair and wore a grey lab coat. She wasn't pleased to see us. I'm very busy, she said, the world is ending… but she took us to an empty looking old kitchen inside, dusty, still used but like something from an old photo…She showed us where we could get a drink of water and make a sandwich. She went away. We sat at the table too exhausted and relieved to speak." Thistle sounded tired as she described this.

"Later she came back. 'I'm not sure if it will happen,' she said, and took us to a bare room with bunks and old grey blankets. 'Lie down here…put blankets over you and keep the windows covered,' she said. She closed some wooden shutters, pulled down blinds and drew thick curtains that were made of more old blankets. 'I have to monitor this, don't go outside,' she said." Raven leaned down and stroked Magda's fur.

"We were so tired, we lay down on the bunks and fell asleep so deeply we could have been unconscious."

Cassie's hands were cold with sweat from the strangeness of the story. Her parents were still, their eyes focused on a distant time, seeing the events of that day. "So what happened?"

"We woke…how much later, we don't know. There was a roaring sound and an immensely bright light came through the cracks at the edge of the window. We felt heat through the shutters, through the glass and the curtains," said Thistle.

"The next moment there was an almighty boom. The window smashed inside the shutters, and the shutters flew open. A flash of light lit every detail of the room."

"We think it knocked us out," said Thistle. Both she and Raven fell silent.

Cassie watched their faces, unable to interject an encouragement to continue speaking.

"We don't know how long we were unconscious."

"It could have been quite a long time…"

"It's one of the things we don't know."

"When we woke up we felt as if we'd been through a tumble dryer," said Thistle.

"What's that?" asked Cassie. There were lots of things in this tale that were unfamiliar.

"Oh, an old thing they used to have when we were young. Hot, and turning things over and over inside a drum…they used them to dry clothes."

"Didn't they know about washing lines?" thought Cassie.

"…dizzy, sick, and sore in the heads. And no closer to home. We opened the bunk room door. We smelled singed wood. The kitchen window had blown in, there was glass all over the floor, and everything in the room was broken; furniture, china, you name it. We went outside. Every tree in sight was lying down, blackened but not burnt up. We ran to the observatory and went in. The woman lay on the floor, her face singed, dried blood in her ears. We picked her up and carried her to the bunk, washed her face, made her as comfortable as we could. We were only sixteen…" Thistle's voice faded.

What happened? Did she die?"

"Eventually she woke. She was blinded by the flash. She must have been looking through her telescope. She couldn't hear. We didn't know what to do. There was a CB radio—"

"What's that?" asked Cassie again.

"Sort of like one of those perso-text things, but you talk into it."

"Like a telephone machine?"

"A little."

Raven took up the story again. "The radio had no signal. We fed the woman from tinned food and water we found in bottles in the pantry. We tried to clean the place up a bit."

"She didn't die. For days she couldn't see or hear, but she talked. At first she only said, 'Go, go,' when she knew we were there; then after a couple of days her hearing began to return. Then the radio made some noises…a voice came through, very faintly."

"Bad news," interupted Raven.

"It was the Disaster," said Cassie.

"Yes," Thistle continued. "The voice said that Walagu was destroyed, turned inside out into nothing but a crater. Stirling was flattened too. You know about all the horrible things that happened."

"And…you came from near Stirling, and from Walagu."
Her parents nodded.

Broken glass crunched as Ivan approached the steel door. Close up the building was weirder than ever, an arrangement of squat masonry cubes painted with peeling grey, one of them domed. It looked deserted. His knock clanged hollowly on the steel.

Immediately a voice said, "Who's there?" and the door opened wide.

CHAPTER EIGHT

IN THE WILDERNESS

Because he had not expected the door to open at all, Ivan was very surprised. He took a step back. In the doorway stood an old woman with long white hair. Her eyes were hidden by dark glasses and she wore a grey lab coat.

"It's about time," she said.

"What?"

"I'm sorry, I meant I haven't had a visitor for a long time. Please come in."

Ivan was still too surprised to reply properly.

"I'm very busy, but visitors are always welcome," said the woman, standing aside so Ivan could enter the building.

"What is this place?"

"The Observatory."

Ivan knew there was a big telescope in the hills near O'Malley, but he had surely not walked that far, and the O'Malley observatory was much bigger. This was tiny; smaller than a house. Just a couple of boxy rooms and a domed observatory smaller than a garage, which looked like a scoop of ice cream placed in a box.

"I am professor Fenella Carter. And you are...?"

"Ivan Williams."

"Where have you come from?

"Willowvale."

The professor stopped short, blocking the corridor. "Which one?" She turned to face Ivan. Her dark glasses hid her eyes so that he had no way of accurately gauging her expression.

"What do you mean?"

"I mean," said the professor slowly and clearly, as if Ivan was a bit deaf, "do you come from the Willowvale that had the Disaster, or the one that did not?"

Ivan thought he had been surprised when he first saw the professor, but the astonishment he experienced now was much greater. He opened and shut his mouth several times without succeeding in making a sound.

"Well?"

"I come from the Willowvale without the Disaster."

"Aha. So you know about the other one."

Ivan stopped mentally in his tracks again. Was there any reason to conceal this knowledge from her?

"Who are you?" he asked.

"I told you. Professor Fenella Carter."

"That's not enough."

"They call me…if they know I exist…the Blind Astronomer. I like to think of myself as an artist, too."

Both of those were impossible, Ivan thought.

"To which Willowvale do you wish to go?" asked the professor.

"At the moment I just want a drink of water and a rest, please. I'm a bit lost. And we have to contact the Fire Service. There's smoke in the hills—a bushfire."

"All in good time, everyone who comes here is a bit lost," said the professor. "First, answer my question. To which Willowvale do you want to go?"

"Is there a choice?"

"Yes, young man, there is."

"How can there be?"

"Well, to cut a long story short, we are at the point where these two worlds intersect. I can tell you how to get to either of them."

The professor led the way into a kitchen which gave Ivan the impression that it had not been used for some years, despite the fact that dirty plates lay on the draining board and there was an old-fashioned kettle on the ancient gas stove. The room's walls were painted an institutional grey. The window was barred, and decorated (if the word was appropriate) with curtains in a pattern like ancient lino flooring in grey, yellow and dusty red. Benches and sinks were made of dull zinc, and the oven handle was draped with checked tea towels, greyed over their original colours. A wobbly wooden table, inexpertly repaired, with a scratched laminex top in a pattern meant to imitate marble stood against one wall; a doorway led into a pantry with tins arranged on shelves; there was a fridge that looked as though it was held together by old souvenir magnets. Several wooden chairs that had been roughly mended after a serious breakage stood around the table. An easel was set up in a corner with a large abstract painting on it; a side table was spread with paints, brushes and a well-used palette made from an old hubcap. There was a smell of linseed oil. Everything was covered in a layer of dust, with finger marks indicating recent use, despite the neglected appearance of the room.

"Welcome," said the professor. "Please sit down and I'll get you a cup of tea."

"Thank you," said Ivan.

"Don't forget, I need to know which Willowvale is your destination before I can tell you how to get there."

"It's not that easy," Ivan said.

The professor sighed, and went to the sink, where she filled a hazy glass jug from the tap. She placed it on the table then went to the cupboard and took out two glasses, equally dirty-looking, and put one in front of Ivan, filling the other for herself.

The question Professor Carter had asked Ivan was a surprisingly difficult one to answer. Of course he wanted to go home to his own Willowvale, but he knew that inside himself the reason he was out here at all was at least partly that he also wanted to go to the other Willowvale.

"I find that most people who end up here want to go to the other one. If they know of it. Whichever the other one is," sid Professor Carter as if he'd spoken his thought aloud.

That didn't make the decision any easier. "I told my parents I'd be home by Sunday night."

"And?"

"I don't want to be missed. I got lost for nearly a week last year and I know how hard it was for my parents."

"Lost in the Willowvale you don't come from, I assume?"

"Yes."

Professor Carter nodded. "I understand. It was impossible to explain to them where you had been. I think I heard of your visit."

Ivan nodded without thinking that the professor could perhaps not see the gesture.

"Well, it's your choice. But it's only Friday afternoon now."

Ivan poured water and drank it in one gulp, not caring that as he swallowed it he remembered the dead spider he'd noticed lying in the bottom of the glass. Friday afternoon? It felt much longer than one afternoon that he'd been wandering in the bush. He wasn't convinced that the professor knew what day it was any more than he did.

Professor Carter was silent, and it seemed to Ivan that she waited for him to ask questions. "If this place is at the intersection of the two—"

"Worlds," she prompted.

"—and you say I can get into either of them from here—"

"Yes,"

"Can…can a person really, truly get into either of the worlds from here?"

Professor Carter reached across the table, picked up the jug and poured herself another glass of water. She took a sip and put the glass down. Ivan found himself wondering once more just how blind she really was. She performed every movement confidently. "Yes, a person can go into either of the worlds from here. I told you that."

"Can you go into either of them, yourself?"

"Theoretically, I can, though my limitations keep me mostly here."

"Suppose…I choose to go to one particular world. Can I come back to this place here, the observatory, and then go into the other?"

"Yes. Providing you can find the observatory again."

It was pretty remote here. Ivan filed at the back of his mind a reminder to ask for specific directions later. The significance of this remark was probably greater than it seemed. He sat looking around the kitchen, at a loss for anything else to say; the professor did not speak. The kitchen did not grow less odd as he became used to it. In the shadows in a corner near a door that led out through the wall opposite the corridor was a strange assemblage of objects mounted on the wall and sitting on a small table. An old telephone like the one Gran and Pop had when he was very, very young, with a circular metal dial with finger holes through which the neatly printed numbers nought to nine were visible; A mobile phone of recent design with a large glass screen, a UHF radio like the one in Dad's work vehicle; a perso-text machine nestled in a pale green plastic charging device with coloured lights not currently flashing, connected to a power point by a candy-striped electrical cord. Ivan stood up and walked across the room to look at this ill-assorted collection. "Do all these phones and things work?"

"Yes."

"All the time? Are they working now?"

"Most of the time. Our electricity supply is not entirely reliable and sometimes there are problems with the phone lines, or the communication towers. As I said, it's very remote here."

"So can you contact people in my world, or in the other one, any time you want to?"

"As I said, mostly, yes."

"Suppose…I want to go to one particular version of the world…but I want to contact someone in the other world, before I leave…can I do that?"

"Yes, you may."

Ivan began to find Professor Carter's repeated affirmatives disturbing. He was used to most answers being "no". He was grateful that the professor was happy to answer his questions without telling him they were silly; nevertheless, it was unnerving. Remembering the ribbon of smoke he'd seen rising from the hills, he said, "We need to call the fire brigade first."

"Which one?"

"What do you mean?"

"I mean, which world were you in when you saw it?"

"The one I came from, of course."

"How can you be sure?"

"You told me that this place is at the point where the two worlds meet. I must have been in my own world when I arrived here."

"Yes, you are correct." The professor poured herself another glass of water. She had evidently forgotten about the promised cup of tea. "Probably."

"So, we should call them in my world."

"Go outside and see whether the smoke is still there, or worse."

Ivan wearily stood up, feeling all the scratches and aches of his journey, left the kitchen, and followed the hallway to the outside door. As he stepped through, the door closed with a clang before he thought to prop it open with a stone, or check that that lock was unlatched. Mentally shrugging and supposing he would have to knock again when he returned, he found a faint footpath like the wallaby trails he'd followed at the beginning of his journey, which led to a rocky outcrop from which the surrounding country was visible in every direction. The storm clouds had moved away and a breeze played about the rocks. There was no sign of smoke at all. Puzzled, he returned to the building. The door was locked. He knocked. As before, almost immediately it was opened by the professor, who was holding a teapot in her hand.

"There's no fire now," Ivan said.

"Who are you? Come in, I'm just making a cup of tea," she said, not standing aside for Ivan to enter.

"Ivan Williams. I was here a few minutes ago. I went out to check for smoke in the hills."

"It's a long time since I had a visitor. Come in, and welcome. What was your name again? How do you do? I am Professor Fenella Carter." Again, the professor led the way along the dark corridor to the kitchen. Ivan was relieved to see that the kitchen was exactly as before. His backpack was where he'd left it slumped against a chair, and the two glasses and jug stood on the table. Two mugs had been put on the table and the kettle whistled distressingly.

"Please sit down. Have a cup of tea. What was your name again? How did you find me?" said Professor Carter, taking the kettle from the heat and pouring boiling water into the teapot.

"I was here a few minutes ago. Ivan. I went outside to check for smoke. Don't you remember? The smoke's gone and the storm clouds have moved away. I must have made a mistake about a bushfire."

The professor stopped pouring tea and gazed upwards as if inspecting a corner of the ceiling through her dark glasses. "Ah. Forgive me. You must have gone out into the other world, not the one you came from," she said. "That would account for two things: one, that I forgot you. I do apologize. The switch is disorienting. Two: the lack of smoke. There is no fire in the world you went to just now. Do you take milk?"

Ivan thought the milk here would be sour. "No, thank you. So what should we do? The fire could turn nasty in my world."

"It's good that the fire is in your world. Fire fighting services are much better there. Someone else has probably called them already. No need to worry." She turned her face directly toward Ivan. "So, have you decided yet to which world you wish to go?"

"Can I come back here and go to the other one?"

"As I said, if you can find your way back here."

"And can we really contact either world from here? Can I send a message to my friends?"

"You may certainly try, though as you must know, communications in that world are not particularly reliable."

Ivan felt a surge of optimism that lifted his mood more than he could have expected when he began this journey. There was a way through. He could see Cassie and Wilfred again. Phil and all the problems he was about to cause could be sent back...

"Do your friends have a phone, or a perso-texts? Do you know their numbers?"

Oh. Ivan drooped. Cassie so much didn't have a phone that she called them telephoning machines.

"Do they have a perso-text? A phone?" repeated the professor.

Ivan racked his brain, but could think of absolutely no way of contacting Cassie. Maybe he could write her a letter?

"You must know someone's number, if you've been there before as you say you have."

"Wilfred!" exclaimed Ivan, jumping out of his chair.

"Excellent. What's his phone number?"

Ivan fell back to his chair. "I don't know."

"His perso-text code?"

"No idea."

The professor went to the communications corner and pulled out from a shelf below the table an enormous book, which she thumped onto the kitchen table, narrowly missing the teapot. "You can look it up in the codebook."

That was good, except— "I don't know his surname."

"There are other ways," said the professor showing the first sign of exasperation. "It's cross-referenced. His address. His profession…"

"He's a school kid. Is that a profession? He lives in the southern suburbs of O'Malley."

"His parents' professions?"

Ivan didn't know. "His mother has a lot of things. They live in a nice house."

"You're remarkably ignorant about this friend," sighed the professor.

"His mother's name is Berenice."

"Well. Lucky it's an unusual name. You'll have to look through the first name listing in all the southern suburbs until you find her."

Ivan wasn't keen on speaking to Wilfred's spiky mother, but this seemed to be the only option; laboriously searching the confusing cross-referenced system of the codebook for any listing. The afternoon wore on, the tea cooled in his mug. He found nothing. It was getting late. I have to find Wilfred's code, he thought, and at that moment saw an entry in the book: Kenaway, Berenice: phone 012 3 45 67, perso-text AB89C01: then a symbol which Ivan's study of the codebook told him meant "others in the same household". He followed the reference there to another page and at last found Kenaway, Wilfred: and a perso-text code. Ivan ripped a piece of old newspaper from the professor's art table, grabbed a pencil and scrawled down Wilfred's perso-text code, and as an afterthought, Berenice's phone number. Rushing to the communications table he picked the perso-text from its cradle. Trying not to fumble, he entered Wilfred's code, and hoping he was doing it correctly, began a message.

Ivan here.

His mind went blank. What could he say?

I think I can come back.

Hurriedly Ivan added the words *old weird observatory somewhere west of Stirling*. He turned the handle on the side of the machine, as he'd seen Wilfred do last year when they first met. The perso-text machine made a musical sound and flashed a rapid pattern of coloured lights across its edge.

Ivan shoved the perso-text back onto its recharge cradle and the piece of paint-stained newspaper with the code into his pocket. The professor came up to him and shook him warmly by the hand. "It's been a pleasure meeting you, um—"

"Ivan," prompted Ivan.

"Well, have a nice trip, goodbye," said the professor and before he knew what had happened, Ivan found himself on the doorstep, his pack on his back, facing the yellow sunlit western side of lines of wooded hills.

CHAPTER NINE
COMMUNICATION

The day after after Cassie heard the story of Thistle and Raven's arrival, she felt a sense of anticlimax. Thistle and Raven went about their ordinary lives. They moved back to the house in town. There was nothing in their tale, romantic and adventurous as it was, to suggest that Penny Williams' idea of them arriving like fugitives from Ivan's world was correct. They'd been lost in the bush by chance, and taken shelter at an observatory somewhere out in the wilderness between Willowvale and O'Malley. There was no way for them to return to their homes because everything was destroyed and their families killed. They told Cassie that they stayed with the astronomer, Fenella Carter. They stayed until she recovered from the impact and injuries she received, though she insisted that their stay was for their sakes. She seemed to cope by maintaining that though she had been at least partly blinded by the intense light of the blast, it was they who were to be pitied, because of the certain loss of their parents, families and homes. She was determined not to let her injury affect her, and spent hours, days, and weeks doggedly teaching herself how to manage. At first she walked tentatively, hands outstretched for balance and location.

The radio crackled and spoke from time to time, but no meaningful communications were received. After about a month, Raven and Thistle told Cassie, she became much more competent, moving confidently around the kitchen and disappearing for hours into the observatory. They were not allowed in there, and Fenella Carter told them that she was adapting her work to her new disability. "We never were sure exactly how much or little she ended up being able to see," said Raven. "She adapted amazingly well, but…well, we simply didn't know. She insisted that she could cope."

Nobody came to the isolated observatory to see if either Fenella or the observatory itself were intact. Thistle and Raven assumed that this was due to the destruction all around. One day Fenella said to them, "It's time you two moved on. There's not enough food for you to stay here. I'll be getting a delivery from O'Malley one of these days, but the food mightn't last till then if you stay."

"Where will we go?"

She said, "I will give you directions to Willowvale. Although there have been no communications from there, I think it would have survived the impact, as the fireball was travelling away from that direction."

"So, she gave us some food and water, and told us how to find our way to Willowvale, and we've been here ever since," Raven said, concluding the story.

"What was it like here?"

"Normal. As normal as it could be under the circumstances…they'd already started building the wall."

That was all very well, but it gave Cassie no clue as to whether her parents came from this world or from Ivan's. In fact, it was a moot point because presumably there was no difference between the worlds at the point when they left their homes. Thistle and Raven themselves appeared to think that there was no mystery at all—that although they had witnessed the disaster at unbelievably close quarters, it had not altered their lives other than by destroying their families and homes.

Cassie tried to get more from them. "What about Mrs Penny Williams' idea that you came over from the other world—the one without the Disaster—that Ivan came from?"

"The only mystery in our lives is what we would have been like if the Disaster had never happened—"

"—in common with everyone else in Willowvale, O'Malley and as far away as I can imagine," her parents said in that odd way they had of finishing each other's sentences.

Cassie, having been told in this way that there were to be no more stories about the past easily extracted from her parents, nor would further questions be willingly answered, went outside and busied herself with the hens, then picked tomatoes and lettuce from the vegetable garden. It was one of those long hot Friday afternoons that seemed to have no purpose of its own, nor allow any purpose in those who experienced it. Cassie could not settle to anything. She felt as if she was waiting for someone to arrive or something to happen, and that there was no point doing anything. Nobody was expected. She wandered about the house, wondering what to do.

Thistle was making soap over an evil-smelling cauldron in the back yard. Raven had gone out, taking the dogs, to visit someone who had cut down a tree that might be good for instrument-making. Flies buzzed against the house windows, trying to get out. Thistle called her, and for a while Cassie helped stir the soap. Soon she wandered away to the front verandah, intending to study for school.

The book had been the property of Willowvale Central School for so long that the school had changed its name twice since the book was new. A purple ink stamp on the endpaper had the names of previous students to whom it had been issued filled in with extremes of neatness and untidiness. It wasn't very interesting other than that. Cassie stared unseeingly at the softly fraying pages. The sounds of the afternoon floated about her. Someone chopping wood. Children playing. A currawong calling. Distant engine sounds. An odd, tinny musical sequence unlike anything her family had ever played. Footsteps and talking outside the garden hedge. A dog barking. Again the faint, unfamiliar music.

"Wilfred!" Cassie jumped up, dropping her book and her pencil and exercise book. She ran inside and took Wilfred's perso-text machine from its hiding-place under her pillow. One of its coloured lights was blinking. A tiny door opened showing the words "new message" below it. Cassie pressed the button with "accept" written on it. Her heart thumped with excitement and dread that she would do something wrong and lose the message, or worse still, ruin the perso-text somehow. The perso-text made a few beeps and with a quiet whirr spat out a short length of paper tape with a series of numbers printed on it.

9.22.5-8.15.20-1-14.5.23-16.5.18.19.20.15-20.5.24.20-23.9.12.6.18.5.4

Cassie remembered the code, and was writing out the message *I've got a new perso text* on a piece of paper when the machine received another message.

Work at Tarzanna's was okay, sometimes even fun. The pay was all right and the people were mostly fine, and all in all Wilfred liked it, particularly as it meant he had money to pay for petrol and other things he wanted.

He had an afternoon shift the day after his visit to Cassie, and was keener than usual to be at work, partly because of the urgent need to get a new perso-text and partly because despite feeling sorry for Berenice after her horrible experience of Thursday night, as Friday wore on she got into a worse and worse mood. Wilfred was glad to have an acceptable reason to get out of the house.

In the staff room after his shift, Wilfred took off his work uniform of polka-dotted shirt, pink trousers and red baseball cap and into his ordinary clothes. Dale was there—a vague friend from school…

"Hey, Wilfred."

"Dale."

"I don't s'pose you know anyone who wants to buy a perso-text, do you? I got a new one for my birthday and my old one is still good."

"I might…how much?"

Dale named an amount less than half the cost of a new perso-text.

"What's wrong with it? Did it fall off the back of a truck?" asked Wilfred, half joking.

"No, mate, of course not. Like I said, new one, birthday, old one's not actually old."

"Does it work?"

"I'll show you if you're really interested."

Wilfred was reluctant to commit himself too soon. Dale was a fast talker. "Yeah, show me. You never know, I might be interested."

Dale pulled a perso-text out of his pocket and handed it to Wilfred.

"Can I send a message?"

"Be my guest."

Wilfred keyed in the code for his old perso-text. What luck. A chance to get another perso-text so soon, and to contact Cassie. It was fortunate that he'd received his pay this afternoon. Dale's price was a good proportion of it, but still, it was a bargain.

I've got a new perso text this number he wrote. "Would you take—" Wilfred named a much lower amount.

Dale hesitated. This gave Wilfred confidence. Dale's hesitation hinted that his story was genuine. If the perso-text was somehow suspect, Wilfred thought Dale would have jumped at the first offer. "I don't know," he said.

"Everyone has one," said Wilfred, "If you don't sell it to me, it might be ages before you find someone who wants it…and it's not as if you had to pay for the new one, seeing as it was a present."

Dale scratched his head and said "Yeah, you're right. I'll meet you halfway."

"I'll buy it when I know it works," said Wilfred, who had the feeling that having got a good deal out of Dale, he should hang onto the upper hand for as long as possible. However, he was worried that he'd been too clever. What if Cassie had forgotten how to operate the perso-text, or didn't recognize the call tune or had lost it or dropped it into the chook water or…

As these thoughts passed through his mind the perso-text that was still officially Dale's signalled an incoming message. Nearly dropping it in excitement, Wilfred pressed the "accept" button and a ribbon of paper message tape emerged from the perso-text.

"See?" said Dale. "It works all right."

Wilfred glanced at the message code. It was definitely from Cassie. *Wilfred Wilfred Wilfred hello,* it said, though the code words were mingled with random letters she must have entered by mistake. He started to enter a reply, but Dale snatched the device. "If you want it, you have to pay." Wilfred handed over the money, straight from his pay envelope. Dale counted it carefully and smiled. "Thanks, mate, enjoy it." Handing the perso-text back to Wilfred, he added, "New girlfriend?"

Wilfred blushed and put it into his pocket, picked up his bag and helmet, and quickly entered a reply to Cassie. Winding the "send" crank clumsily as he went, he entered the main part of the restaurant. It was very like the one he used to work in last year about the time Ivan and Cassie came to O'Malley. The restaurant was brightly lit, with an elaborate arrangement of coloured lights, which illuminated seating booths decorated to resemble a jungle inhabited by gaudily striped tigers, polka-dotted leopards, and crocodiles mysteriously marked with multi-coloured squares. The place was filling up with young people about his age.

Glad to be dressed in his normal clothes, and not required to take orders or carry awkward trays of drink and food through the narrow aisles between the tables, Wilfred headed for the exit. He passed one booth packed with people about his own age, all talking loudly at the same time, except for one. At their centre was a girl of striking appearance dressed flamboyantly in the very latest O'Malley fashion. He'd see her before, quite often. She was usually the liveliest and loudest in the group, but this afternoon, although she was sitting in her usual central place, and the others spoke to her as often as usual, the girl's handsome oval face was unusually serious, and she did not respond to her friends, but sat silently more like a statue than a human being.

As Wilfred passed, his eyes and the girl's met. He gave a half smile. She did not smile, but he felt her eyes follow him through the restaurant. His new perso-text gave a notification. It must have been Cassie. No-one else knew the new code. Wilfred suddenly had the chilling thought that Cassie might have received messages from his mother. He hoped not. The message tape rolled out. It was less incompetently written than the previous message. Walking across the car park to his motor bike, he read it.

Surely if there was a code for exclamation marks, this message would have been so bristling with them that it was dangerous to read. As it was, the message nearly caused Wilfred to drop the new perso-text.

You will never guess what happened I just got a message from Ivan.

What do you mean? replied Wilfred. She must be confused. There was absolutely no way Cassie could have received a perso-text from Ivan. Maybe she meant some other kind of message. Perhaps Ivan had left a letter hidden under a rock for her or perhaps her brother had returned from Ivan's world, bringing a message from there. He turned the ignition key of his motorbike and headed for home. The perso-text tinkled its message-receiving tune as he drove.

Berenice, who appeared to have recovered from her adventure of the night before, was watching television when Wilfred arrived home. The house was if possible tidier than usual. Every surface shone. The carpets were arranged on the floor with geometrical precision. A smell of furniture polish mingled with cooking filled the air. Apricot chicken and apple crumble. It appeared that Berenice's bad mood of the last couple of days had dispersed.

"Hello darling. How was work?"

Wilfred wanted to get to his room and read the new messages. "Okay."

"You must get changed out of that horrible jacket and into respectable clothes. We've got visitors coming for dinner."

Oh no. That meant the pastel trousers with pleats, shirt in a multi-coloured pattern, satin tie and linen jacket that Berenice had given him for his birthday. "Can't I wear my jeans?" Wilfred muttered.

"I heard that. No, you can not. These are special guests and I don't want you to embarrass me."

Wilfred noted that Berenice wore one of her many glamorous cocktail dresses and enough makeup to cover the bruises of last night. That was good. She was moving on. He wondered who the special guests could be. Surely—and here the whole idea of his mother having a boyfriend at all, let alone a new one, intruded. The Rexy fiasco should have discouraged her for a while. It must be some friends of hers from the office where she worked. He hurried to the shower and applied all the personal care substances he could find, all the while trying not to think too much about the evening to come. His mother was strange at times, and annoying, but he loved her and wanted to please her. He sighed at the dazzling pastel-coloured vision that was his reflection in the mirror, put the perso-text into the pocket of his good trousers and went out to the kitchen.

"Darling, you look gorgeous." Berenice patted Wilfred carefully on his recently blow-dried hair. "Can I ask you a favour? Mix up a jug of one of those fancy drinks they sell at Tarzanna's?"

The doorbell rang. Berenice hurried to answer it. Wilfred also hurried, busying himself with bottles of juice and liqueurs, tiny paper umbrellas, crushed ice and candied cherries. He heard voices in what Berenice called the foyer, and Berenice entered the kitchen followed by a tall, heavy man in a baby-blue linen jacket.

"Wilfred, darling, I want you to meet Rex."

CHAPTER TEN

FAMILIES

Wilfred felt himself go cold despite the warm afternoon and his uncomfortable tie and jacket.

"Wilfred. Manners."

He stood open-mouthed.

"Say hello, Wilfred." As he stood opening and shutting his mouth like a goldfish, another person entered the kitchen. "Wilfred. Pull yourself together. I'm so sorry, he's a difficult age. This is Wilfred. Wilfred, say hello to Rex and Jessica."

The man called Rex loomed in front of Wilfred, obscuring Jessica. "Hello, young man." He held out his hand.

Wilfred felt like a small child, both because of his mother's stream of talk and because the visitor was so large. He said hello, didn't shake Rex's hand, tried to get a better view of the girl, and wanted to get out of the situation, all at once.

"He's had a hard day at work," said Berenice. She prodded Wilfred sharply in the ribs, which he took to mean that she wanted him to go and get drinks for the guests.

Dinner was strained from the start, despite the apricot chicken and apple crumble, not to mention wine, which disappeared rapidly. Jessica was silent, looking down at her food but not eating much of it, her hair hanging in front of her face. Wilfred was sure, trying to see her better, that she was the same girl he'd noticed as he left Tarzanna's. She looked as if she was as unhappy about being present at this meal as Wilfred was. There was something dire about being forced to socialize with one's parents' friends, and even worse, their friends' offspring. Rex kept up a stream of nervous conversation which Berenice batted back to him in a distracted manner.

Wilfred was so disturbed by the fact that his mother had asked the man who had beaten her up to the house that he remained as silent as Jessica. He spent the meal watching and trying to work things out. He thought Rex was nervous (and with good reason), while Berenice was the image of a person bursting with something—a plan of some sort—and from experience Wilfred knew it would be an uncomfortable surprise of some kind. Rex looked as if he also had enough knowledge of Berenice to dread this. For a hundredth of a second Wilfred felt a flash of sympathy for him. Wilfred knew the signs: her restlessness, her inattentiveness to conversation except at the most superficial level; the gleam in her eyes and the way she had of starting forward ready to speak, then pulling back with an air of concealing a secret.

The evening crawled on painfully for all the participants except perhaps Berenice. Whenever Wilfred had a reason to leave the table, whether to take plates away or bring in more food (he felt like a waiter even though he wasn't at work), he sneaked into his room to check his perso-text. Cassie's messages were mystifying. It was a disjointed conversation, marred by Cassie's unfamiliarity with the workings of the perso-text, and the fact that Wilfred had to keep returning to the dining room. Between courses he managed to lay out all the paper message tapes on his desk. He took a page from his school folder and a pot of paste, and stuck the messages down, adding punctuation and capitals—a shortcoming of the perso-text coding system was that it lacked punctuation—and wrote his answers between as well as he could recall them. He wanted to understand this conversation. From the start, it went:

—Wilfred Wilfred Wilfred hello(!)

—You will never guess what happened I just got a message from Ivan (!!!!)

Wilfred did not have the paper tapes of his messages, but he knew exactly what he'd said on his way out of the restaurant. —*What do you mean(?)* He seriously regretted the long gap between the sending of this message and reading the next one. Drat and double drat it.

—Ivan sent me a perso text message.

When he saw this now, Wilfred entered a reply as bristling with implied punctuation marks as Cassie's —*How could he(?) Where is he(?) Have you seen him(?)*

She replied immediately —*I don't know I don't know (,) no.*

—*What did he say(?)*

Cassie's reply came quickly. —*He said Ivan here I think I can come back. He also said old weird observatory.*

—*What does that mean(?)*

Tapping footsteps sounded outside Wilfred's room. "Wilfred? Where are you? Where are your manners? Come out and be with our guests."

Your guests, not mine, thought Wilfred. He shut the page of messages inside the folder.

"Leave that perso-text in your room."

As Wilfred left the room, the perso-text registered receipt of another message, but he could not accept or read it.

Berenice hustled everyone into the sitting room for coffee, after-dinner mints and what she called "a nice chat". She still fizzed with tension, which Wilfred would have thought was excitement if the evening had not been so grim. Jessica had not said one word the whole time. Rex was clearly uncomfortable. Wilfred had spoken as little as possible so far, and continued in the same way, putting his energy into watching Rex constantly from under his fringe. He was pleased to see that this had the effect of making Rex sweat more than the warmth of the evening required, and fiddle nervously with his tie.

"Jessica, Wilfred, I'm so pleased to have you here together—"

What was this? A school speech night? Wilfred glanced at Jessica, who stared ahead, her eyes on the recently and perfectly polished coffee table.

"—because this concerns both of you," Berenice continued, beaming like the presenter on a washing powder advertisement.

"Bernie—" Rex started up, knocking over the dish of chocolates. "This is a bad idea."

"We've discussed it, remember. You agreed," said Berenice, touching the makeup-covered bruise on her face with a gesture that could have been deliberate or unconscious. She looked at Wilfred and Jessica, who she had seated next to each other on the couch, and spoke over Rex, who was spluttering inarticulately.

"Jessica, I'm your mother. Wilfred, Rex is your father. We're going to be a family at last." She held her hand out toward them, showing a shiny new ring with a large, glittering pink stone.

CHAPTER ELEVEN
MYSTERIES

—Ivan here I think I can come back old weird observatory somewhere west of Stirling Cassie replied to Ivan's message with trembling excitement. *—I know where it is I will meet you there.* It was frustrating that she couldn't work out the code for exclamation marks, punctuation or capitals.

That she knew the exact location of the observatory was not, of course, strictly true but Cassie was sure she could easily get the information out of her parents. She began to make plans in her head. Ivan didn't reply, which was annoying. While Cassie was feeling annoyed, the perso-text made incoming-message sounds. Her heartbeat, which had calmed, raced again. Ivan's reply! She accepted the message, and Wilfred's message came out of the device.

—I have got a new perso text Wilfred

Cassie was as embarrassed at her disappointment as she would have been if Wilfred had witnessed it. She was very fond of Wilfred. He was one of her very best friends. And really, she wasn't disappointed at all. It was fantastic to hear from Wilfred. At last he'd got another perso-text machine. It had seemed like forever. She was very excited.

—Wilfred wilfred wilfred hello she sent to him. *—You will never guess what happened I just got a message from Ivan*

Almost immediately, equipped with all she could imagine she needed, Cassie headed in the direction from which Thistle and Raven had arrived all those years ago. Her parents didn't know that Cal had been teaching her to drive his motorbike. Seeing as Cal had left without a word to her, she felt no compunction in taking the bike out of the shed that opened onto the back lane, strapping the spare helmet onto the pillion. Ivan would need it.

"Back soon," she'd said to Thistle. It was lucky she'd also thought of borrowing Cal's leather jacket, because in an unbelievable stroke of luck, while she was looking for it in his wardrobe, she'd found the map. Raven and Thistle's map…fallen among the boots at the bottom of the wardrobe. Cal's boots were too big for her, but the luck of finding the map was too fabulous to imagine. It was a hand-drawn sketch on graph paper, notated in what was recognizably both Thistle and Raven's writing in smudgy pencil, hidden in an old folder with *Important* written on it.

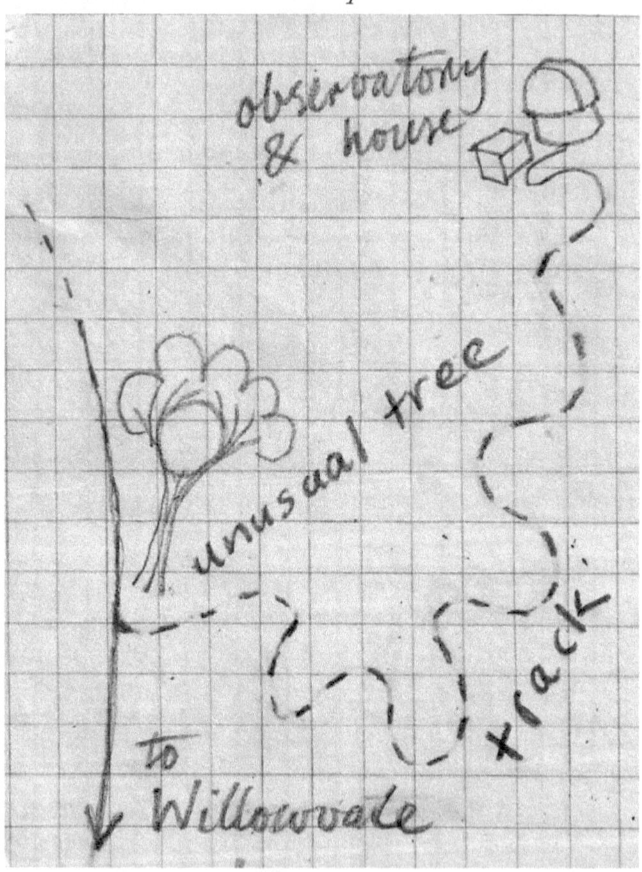

After crossing the river by the bridge near the disused pumping station and water treatment plant, Cassie followed a crumbling road that wound up a steep hill. She had never been there before, despite its proximity to her home. She stopped and consulted the map frequently as she went. It was a pleasant afternoon after the heat and distant thunderstorms of yesterday afternoon.

She came to a straighter section that followed near the top of a ridge with views to the west. A smaller track joined the road she was following, and she stopped to check the map.

The perso-text tinkled. Interesting. How did it get messages out here?

—*What do you mean* asked Wilfred. What did she mean what? Oh, the message from Ivan. It had taken Wilfred an awfully long time to answer. What was he thinking?

—*Ivan sent me a perso text message,* she wrote.

Immediately Wilfred replied with a string of questions. —*How could he where is he have you seen him.* She replied quickly —*I don't know I don't know No.*

—*What did he say,* Wilfred asked.

—*He said - Ivan here I think I can come back. He also said old weird observatory*

—*What does that mean*

Cassie sighed and keyed in —*The message says old weird observatory somewhere west of Stirling. Now I have to go.*

By the time the sun neared the crest of the western hills, Cassie was fairly sure she was near the point where she should leave the faint road that followed an indistinct landform that could have been a valley, if it was more organized. She stopped again to check the map. An arrow indicated the place where the trail left this road near a smudged sketch of an oddly shaped tree, very small but circled several times. *"Trail starts here"* was written next to it.

She scanned the forest beside the road for what felt like many kilometres, looking for a curious tree resembling the sketch. "A tree could easily be gone in that length of time," Cassie warned herself. It was getting to the time of day when she would have to set up camp for the night. She began to worry. Then she saw the tree.

At last. A large, old tree with an odd configuration of limbs that, seen from the correct angle, formed the semblance of a round window with a view of hills and sky through it. An indistinct trail led from next to the tree into the hills; an old fire trail with two ruts made by wheels, more overgrown than the road she was on, but easy enough to follow. "That's good," Cassie said to herself.

It felt different here. More enclosed. More mysterious. "This is where

Raven and Thistle came from! I'm sure of it." A little way along the trail she consulted the map again. The route was marked with a wiggly dotted line that continued for some kilometres. Now that she'd found it, the time of day was less urgent. *I'll stop and camp at the first good place I see*, she said to herself. This was good. Everything was going well. This expedition was going to be a huge success. She'd find Ivan, and the observatory where the two worlds met, and get Pip back.

The track became rougher, more overgrown and barred with fallen branches. It was not easy to keep the bike upright, and she had to dismount and walk at times. Coming down a curve that crossed a small creek, Cassie saw a place that would do for a campsite. "I'll go to the top of this rise and take a look around before I decide," she thought. The trail wound on as before, up the hill. The sun was hidden behind the side of the gully, rays from its edge reddening the leaves at the top of the opposite ridge so that they resembled flames. One more bend and she'd be at the top.

It was amazing. The vegetation changed at the crest of the ridge. Gone was the mature forest filled in with flowering bushes and ferny gullies. Ahead lay a plateau littered with fallen, burnt trees, carbon worn off them in charcoaly piles, leaving silver-grey wood. Between them were rose saplings, too small to make a canopy, their narrow shadows writhing over the fallen trees. Occasional large boulders broke the pattern of devastation and regeneration. The trail wound around fallen trees in a painfully slow line of yellow sand grown through with flowering thistles. On a far hill stood a small human-made structure. The observatory, exactly as Raven and Thistle had described it, lit a fiery pink by the setting sun. Cassie rode for a short distance then stopped the bike and stared.

The perso-text message-received tune was weaker than before. — *Where?* asked Wilfred, continuing their disjointed conversation.

—*I am meeting him I have found the observatory*

She rode a little further. Her moving shadow joined and separated from the tree shadows, which moved in a breeze that bent the slim trees and made them dance eerily. The observatory was as far away as ever, flashing in and out of view.

Something moved among the shadows. Cassie decided she would definitely camp down in the gully. It was getting dark quickly now. The unwelcoming scene made her nervous. —*I will come and find you* answered Wilfred while Cassie was turning the bike. Probably a wallaby, she thought, hoping it wasn't a wild dog. She didn't read the message. She put the bike into gear and moved slowly back down the track. Before she had travelled far the sun finally disappeared behind the hills, leaving a warm blue twilight. She read Wilfred's latest message in the last of the light, and sent him one: —*No, it is too late. It is dark now.*

Some time in the night, Cassie woke and could see nothing inside her makeshift tent. She saw two triangles of lighter darkness, one at her feet, the other at her head, that marked the ends of her shelter. She drew the blanket close around her and tried to go back to sleep. A stick cracked nearby. Those wallabies must have come close in curiosity. She lay quiet, half scared, heart thumping. There were more rustlings and the snap of twigs then a clatter as the wallaby trod on her enamelled metal plate.

"Shit," said the wallaby.

Cassie sat up, her head hitting the tarpaulin that formed the shelter. It didn't hurt, but it made a clearly audible noise.

"Who's there? I've got…I've got a gun," she said loudly.

There were sounds of tripping and falling. The plate would be well and truly dented now. "Ow."

"I'm warning you," said Cassie, wishing she really did have something to defend herself with. She struggled out of the blanket and scrambled out through the farthest end of the tent, feeling in her pocket for the bike keys. The person did not answer. Perhaps he (the voice had sounded like a "he") was winded. "Don't try anything," she said, making her voice gruff.

The person could be heard struggling to his feet. It was so dark under the thick tree canopy in the gully that he was nothing more than a shadow. He looked smaller than he sounded. Cassie backed away, but the bike was between her and the shadowy person. To move away from him meant moving further from the bike. She felt on the ground for a stick to defend herself with, but none came to hand.

Without warning, a light flashed on, like the headlight of a miniature motorbike. An electric torch. Cassie had heard of them, but never seen one. The person directed it at Cassie's face so all she could see was the small bright circle of light like a dazzling moon, surrounded by what now became inky darkness. "Stop that," she said, shielding her eyes.

"Cassie? Is it really you?"

Cassie stood rooted to the ground like one of the trees that surrounded her.

"Cassie? What are you doing here? Is it you? What are you doing here? It can't be true."

"Ivan?"

Ivan redirected the torch beam, which waved wildly across the trees. Cassie stood, breathing fast, feeling suddenly cold.

Ivan must have realized that she hadn't yet been able to see him properly, for he shone the torch upwards at his own face, then turned it off, perhaps thinking the uplighting would make him a frightening sight.

Cassie said in a slow voice, "It is really you. Isn't it?" She stepped carefully around the tent. Now he was a dark shape again, mixed up with the velvety night.

"It's definitely me," said Ivan before his voice was lost, as Cassie squeezed him in a huge hug. "I don't understand," he said. "How can you be here?"

Cassie thought a more pertinent question was, how did Ivan come to be in her world, but she said, "Ivan! I thought I'd never see you again!" She squeezed him even more tightly, until he protested, though he was at the same time not attempting to get away. She put her hand up to his cheek, then took it away. He might not like that kind of…kind of what?

"Oh, Cassie, I'm so glad to see you," Ivan said, and kissed her so lightly on the lips she wasn't sure it had happened. He drew back as if he, too, was unsure of the reaction that would follow.

Cassie hugged Ivan once more then released him and took his hand. "I told you I'd find you," she said.

"No, you didn't," said Ivan.

"But you've got a perso-text. You sent me a message."

"It's not mine. I don't have it. That's the one up at the observatory, Professor Carter's one…I only had time to send the message…but it was to Wilfred. How did you get it? Is Wilfred here too?"

"I wish he was…he gave this one to me so we could keep in touch."

"Oh."

"Last week. It's too complicated to explain."

"I'm too tired to understand anything anyway."

It was too much. Wilfred had always wanted a father, wondered what his father was like, had an imaginary picture of his father in his mind. Not this father. Not a ready-made sister with an attitude problem, the details of whose existence were still unexplained. Ignoring the words someone was speaking, which he couldn't take in anyway—every word merged and muddled with its neighbours into a meaningless jumble —he left the room.

Wilfred was on his motorbike and starting to move when the bike jolted and swayed. He stopped and twisted round to see the cause, and nearly fell over. Jessica was on the pillion seat, looking fierce.

Jessica leaned forward and said something, but her words were fuzzy and grey.

"What?"

"I can't stand it either," she repeated. "Let me come." Jessica unhooked the spare helmet from the seat and put it on.

What the heck? It was easier than arguing. Wilfred engaged first gear and drove.

Out of O'Malley, away from Berenice and Rex. It must all be some horrible mistake. Rex couldn't be his father. Wilfred had so much to think about that he didn't notice where he drove. Houses and street lights gave way to rural subdivisions. The bright lights of the Lakeview Hotel and World's Biggest Water Slide appeared. Wilfred felt knocking on his helmet.

"Stop!" shouted Jessica.

They pulled up at the lookout. The illuminated water slide wriggled through the darkness to the lake where thrillseekers plunged screaming from the tube, breaking the surface of the water into shards of reflected light. Music floated across from the hotel. Coloured search lights cut across the sky. Wilfred and Jessica stood at the lookout rail watching the scene.

"You're just as disgusted as I am," said Jessica. It could have been a statement or a question.

"Yes."

"They deserve each other."

"Maybe." Wilfred was not entirely convinced of this.

"But it's not fair on us."

"We don't deserve each other," said Wilfred without thinking.

There was a brief pause. Jessica laughed. "I actually quite like the idea of having a brother. Call me Jess. Everyone except…your…our…mother already does. Oh shit. I've already got a mother back in Willowvale. I don't want yours. She's psycho. I want mine. The one I've always had."

"I'm not too keen on your father either."

"Do you think it's true?"

"I don't know. Do we look alike?"

"I hope not."

Something Jess had said a moment before chose this moment to penetrate far enough through the armour of shock Wilfred was feeling to register in his mind. "You're from Willowvale? What's your last name?"

"Bagshaw."

This time Wilfred really was rendered speechless. He looked toward Jess. Her face was obscured by the coloured lights that flashed from the hotel and he hadn't paid enough attention to her before to really notice her appearance. She did have straight blonde hair and blue eyes like his. No. It couldn't be true. Rex Bagshaw, the ex-president of Willowvale couldn't be his father. Berenice couldn't be Jess' mother. Lots of people had straight blonde hair and blue eyes. His legs felt shaky. He felt faint. He sat down abruptly on the kerb. He had not recognized Rex this evening because he'd not seen him close up before, but Rex Bagshaw's name was everywhere in Willowvale last year when the adventure happened. The virtual dictator of the town, who'd been deposed and had run away with his tail between his legs. Wilfred might not have seen Rex Bagshaw, but he'd surely heard of him. He opened his mouth to say, "it can't be," but no sound came out.

"I'm not that keen, as you put it, on Daddy myself at the moment," said Jess quietly. "I'm not keen on O'Malley. I want to go home to Willowvale and see Mother."

Wilfred sat with his head in his hands. Jess sobbed once, then blew her nose noisily.

"So what can we do?"

"Cracked granite, I don't know."

As they stared blankly at the darkness that contained the lake, Wilfred's perso-text notified an incoming message. He jumped. Probably Mum. He had no intention of talking to her. No. It couldn't be her. She wouldn't know his new code. He accepted the message. Maybe it was Cassie. He'd forgotten her in the drama of the evening.

—mate hows the perso text want to come down town tonight dale.

Wilfred had no interest in going to town with Dale, but was grateful that he'd reminded him about Cassie.

"Cassie! I have to find her and Ivan." He jumped up. What was it she'd said? He tried to remember. Observatory…somewhere…Stirling…

"Did you say Cassie?"

"What?" Wilfred didn't realize he'd spoken aloud.

"Cassie who?"

"I don't know her last name."

"Where's she from?"

"I have to find her. Now." But Jess had interrupted his train of thought. Observatory… West… Weird… Somewhere…

"You should take me to Willowvale. I want to go. You don't have anything better to do, no point going home."

"Shut up! Cassie might be in trouble."

"I don't care about Cassie, whoever she is. I'm the one in trouble."

Wilfred felt like leaving Jess right here.

CHAPTER TWELVE
IT'S COMPLICATED

Jess perched on the pillion seat trying to hold on without too much contact with Wilfred. Not that she found him repulsive, nor was she particularly shocked at being told that he was her brother. She knew now he was the anonymous caller of the other night, but that didn't bother her. She was wary of Wilfred because she was sure he didn't want to go to Willowvale, and she'd railroaded him into taking her. It was sort of nice of him to do so, but his back looked angry, and unpredictable tempers undeniably ran in the family, if he was indeed her brother.

They passed the ruins of Stirling, depressing in the darkness. Not far now. Jess felt apprehensive about what she'd say to Mother, and how Mother would react to seeing her after all that had happened. She must have known all along, of course, that Jess wasn't her child. Jess let her mind wander to the future and was not paying attention to the surroundings when she realized that they had left the main road and were driving on a rougher dirt road that led down toward the river. She tapped Wilfred's shoulder. He ignored her. Jess became a little alarmed. Where were they going? What was happening? She was used to being in control of the situation. Most people ended up doing what she wanted; some because of her manner, some her looks, and Daddy because she was his little princess. If this was a taste of what it was like to have a sibling, she didn't like it. The dirt road crossed a causeway and climbed a winding route. She tapped Wilfred's shoulder again, harder, but he did not react. Jess became more and more worried. She had never before been in a situation where she had so little control, except for that awful day when she and Daddy left Willowvale. She clutched Wilfred's back and hoped he wasn't going to do anything stupid. It was impossible to work out where they were, but it certainly wasn't Willowvale.

Sunlight dotted through trees, waking Cassie and Ivan to the joyful calls of birds. They sat on a fallen log, looking down the gully, which faced the morning sun. Whipbirds made their duets; rays of light climbed down the misty air. Ivan still couldn't quite believe his luck in finding Cassie and that she was as pleased to see him as he was to see her.

"I don't understand why you're here," Ivan said several times.

"It's really much too complicated to explain."

Ivan knew how he came to be here, to this place, to this gully. He was confused about exactly which world he and Cassie were in right now. At a logical level he knew he must be in Cassie's world; how else could they be together? But the similarity of the landscape and the disorientation of his last twenty-four hours fought logic in his mind. He said, however, "I'm intelligent. I've got plenty of time. You can explain it to me."

"That may well be true," said Cassie, sounding exactly like her father, "but finding you is like an unexpected bonus in the scheme of things. I'm on a quest—"

"Let me guess—"

"—to get Pip back."

"—to find Phil. I know exactly where he is right now, and I doubt you'll find it easy to get him back."

Cassie put her elbows on her knees, her chin in her hands and Ivan saw her face close up like a sea anemone that's been touched.

"I know. I'm trying to be balanced about it, but I don't want to never see him again. I...he's my brother. I care about him."

Ivan heard real sadness in her voice. Cassie became very quiet. "Is something else wrong too?" he asked.

"It's Wilfred. I saw him the other day. We had an argument. About Pip."

"Oh."

"I'd like to see him again and sort it out. I've been thinking about what he said."

"So, when can you see him again?" Ivan sidled along the log and put his arm over her shoulder.

Cassie sat bolt upright. "I can see Wilfred—I could see him today. I might see him soon." Ivan looked around, expecting to see Wilfred coming up the fire trail, then realized he'd misunderstood. Cassie took a tangle of perso-text tape out of her pocket. "You know how impulsive he is. He sent me a message. He might be here any moment. Or maybe we should go and look for him." She riffled through the paper tapes until she found the one she wanted. "Look!"

Ivan took the tape.

9-25.9.12.12-13.15.13.5-1.14.4.6.9.15.4-25.15.21

"I can't read it."

Cassie took the tape and put it back into her pocket. "It says, *I will come and find you.*"

"But—"

"I told him what you said about the observatory. He's probably been bumbling around some overgrown fire trail all night. I should have believed him when he said he'd come."

"Has he sent any more messages? He's probably fast asleep at home in his bed."

"He sent me this too." Cassie brought out the rat's nest of paper again.

"Just tell me what it says."

"He said things were strange and he had to get away. There's something odd going on with his mother. I don't know what. He rushed back on Thursday night because of some messages she sent."

Ivan felt uncomfortable. He didn't want to go chasing after Wilfred. Much as he would have liked to see him, Ivan wanted Cassie to himself for as long as possible. "I thought we could go up to the observatory...I'll explain about it."

"I know all about the observatory. Raven and Thistle told me."

Ivan was surprised, but this was, he guessed, a short version of the long story Cassie hadn't told him earlier. "—then you could come to my place, and see Phil, and, besides—"

"What?"

"My parents are probably worrying."

"Didn't you tell them you were coming out here?"

"Yeah, sort of, but—"

"There's no point worrying about that right now."

"Well, I want to get to the observatory and call my parents or they'll think I'm lost or caught in a bushfire or something. They worry."

"When are they expecting you home?"

"Sunday night. Tonight." Ivan still wasn't sure how long he'd been wandering in the bush.

"Silly. It's only Saturday morning now. You've got plenty of time. And there's no bushfire. Look. I don't know why you're worrying, Ivan."

Ivan peered through the leaves above. Scattered glimpses of the sky were clear and bright. Had he really been so sick and confused that less time had passed in his mind than had in reality? He still felt a bit odd in the stomach, and rather weak. It was possible.

"I still want to go to the observatory."

"Of course. We have to get into your world to find Pip."

It was unusual for Jess to wake up early, but really, sleeping on the ground with a helmet for a pillow and Wilfred's leather jacket, which he'd lent less out of kindness than guilt, for a blanket, had been so uncomfortable that she was glad for an excuse to get up. First light crept into the sky. Wilfred sat nearby, his arms hugged across his chest.

"Where are we?" said Jess. She'd given up being angry with Wilfred. The screaming argument last night night when he finally stopped and wouldn't admit he was lost was too exhausting to repeat.

"I've worked it out. This road goes back to Willowvale," said Wilfred, pointing down the road, but not looking at her.

Jess sighed. "And?"

"Either her perso-text has gone flat or she's ignoring me."

There was no point beating around the bush, metaphorically speaking. Jess had a feeling there'd be plenty of it in real life soon. "Is this Cassie the Cassie from Willowvale? Cassie Reinhardt?"

Wilfred nodded.

Jess didn't want to ask questions about Cassie. "*I know her,*" she wanted to say, "*I can't stand her,*" but she'd forgotten why, or it didn't matter right now, so she said nothing. "*Why are we here?*" she wanted to say, and "*Why aren't we going to Willowvale?*"

In tangential response to the question Jess had not asked, Wilfred said, "It's hard to explain. I want to take you to Willowvale, Jess, but this is important. I have to find Cassie. She might need help."

Jess felt anger swelling in her again. She was important too. She needed help too. She had never felt so helpless in her whole life. She stood up and walked away from Wilfred.

They had stopped beneath a massive old tree—one that had survived the Disaster while those around it had not. The younger trees around made a thick forest underfilled with shrubs. Jess walked slowly, not paying much attention to her surroundings. Everything was too confusing to bother.

She heard the sound of a motorbike engine. He'd better not leave without her or she would have good reason to be angry; stuck in the bush, not knowing where she was. With a stab of fear, Jess automatically felt for her perso-text to call for help, then grunted in frustration when she remembered she'd left it at Berenice's house, in her bag. The engine noise came from the wrong direction. Was it an echo? Maybe a lyrebird. Looking more closely, Jess realized she was on a neglected old fire trail. "Wilfred! Don't you dare leave without me!" She hurried back toward the place where she'd last seen him. The trail was quite obvious now that she paid attention. "Wilfred …don't you dare! You come back!"

The sight of a bike catching up with her, coming from the wrong direction was so unexpected that Jess screamed. That the driver was Cassie Reinhart did not surprise her as much as it might have. Wilfred came running.

"What's she doing here?" were Cassie's first words.

Cassie's passenger dismounted and took off his helmet. A mousy-haired, skinny boy a bit younger than her, grey with dirt. "Who's he?" said Jess.

"Ivan!" Wilfred galloped up to the boy. Their greeting would have been amusing if everything wasn't so fully weird.

Next thing Jess knew, they were all riding up the overgrown track through regenerated Disaster-felled forest. Now too intrigued to be angry, Jess felt surreally like an interloper and a fly on the wall. Cassie and the boy with the mousy hair led the way. Ivan. Seeing Cassie again reminded Jess of Pip. She'd thought for a moment it was him with Cassie. Jess still had a bit of a crush on him, despite the fact that his family had been instrumental in Daddy losing everything. Oh yeah, she remembered. That was why she couldn't stand Cassie. Jess hadn't had a proper look at Ivan. She felt that she should have known him but his rather nondescript appearance rang no bells in her memory. He'd said something earlier about Willowvale, but if he was from Willowvale, she should know him.

Wilfred and Cassie parked the bikes outside a tiny, abandoned-looking observatory next to a small house that was almost completely cubical. Dust swirled around the tyres as they dismounted. The strange block-shaped buildings offered no shade.

The other three huddled in conversation on the doorstep of a blocky grey building. They were talking about her. She could tell.

"We have to tell her," said Wilfred, "we can't just leave her here."

"What am I? A pet dog? A piece of furniture?" Jess went closer.

Cassie was saying, "Yeah, but you can't trust her."

Wilfred, who had been showing every sign of infatuation with Cassie, unexpectedly defended Jess, saying, "You have to trust her. She's my sister."

Everything was a long story, Jess thought, but nobody was bothering to tell any of the stories to her. The unusual feeling of everything being out of control continued. She supposed she had choices but they were unattractive, or she didn't know what they were at all. She could perso-text to Daddy, if she had her bag.

"She's my sister," said Wilfred again.

"What?" said Ivan.

"That's preposterous. She can't be," said Cassie.

"Well I am," said Jess, "so get over it."

"Is this true?" Ivan asked Wilfred. "How can it be?"

"I never knew a thing about it until last night," said Wilfred.

"But how?" said Cassie. "It can't be true. It's impossible."

"They sprung it on both of us," said Wilfred. "There's no reason not to believe them."

"If it's a shock for you, imagine how it is for us," said Jess.

Ivan said, "They do look alike."

"I guess so," said Cassie, staring critically from Jess to Wilfred and back. "But it's irrelevant. We have to get Ivan home and find Pip." Jess remembered that was one of the other reasons she disliked Cassie. Cassie was so bossy.

Ivan knocked on the door. There was a hollow sound to the knock, and a pause so long that Jess thought there would be no answer. Cassie lifted her hand to knock again, and Ivan turned to check out the domed observatory when the door opened a crack. Jess saw a bony hand holding tightly to the door and heard a woman's voice, quavering uncertainly. "What do you want? It's not convenient." Jess could not see her, other than the gaunt hand on the door. "I'm sick. Go away."

The door opened and Jess saw a crone-like woman with crazy white hair and a shapeless grey coat, her eyes hidden in dark glasses.

"Professor Carter…" Ivan started to say.

"Ivan. It's you again. I thought you'd gone home. You'd better introduce me to your friends, who came out of nowhere." Suddenly the woman sounded rational, though she looked as sick as she had said.

"Sorry. Professor Fenella Carter, this is Wilfred, Cassie and Jess."

The professor shakily offered her hand to each in a gesture that did not connect with theirs. Jess felt more and more agitated. This woman was unnerving. Her opaque glasses hinted that she was blind; if she wasn't blind they must have impeded her vision, yet either way she showed no sign of the tentativeness that Jess would have associated with blindness. This whole situation was ridiculous. "I'm only here because Wilfred's taking me to Willowvale," Jess interrupted.

The woman turned her black-lensed gaze on Jess. "You're from Willowvale? Which one?"

"The only one," said Jess. She was fed up with the situation. She wanted to go home and see Mother, and not feel confused and lost.

Professor Carter opened her mouth to reply, but at that moment her hand relaxed its grip on the door, there was a series of thumps and a crash. The door thudded shut.

"The back door," said Ivan, and dashed 'round the corner of the building, followed by Cassie and Wilfred. Jess, a moment behind, followed, picking her way over weeds in the high heeled shoes she was tired of; over charred woodwork and broken glass, to another door sheltered by a small porch. She followed the others through a dingy kitchen piled with dirty dishes and into a shadowy hallway. Wilfred, Ivan and Cassie were bent over the fallen figure of the woman. Light, perhaps from a faulty kitchen fitting that Jess couldn't see, flickered unnervingly.

CHAPTER THIRTEEN
INSTABILITY

The professor, as Ivan called the old woman, lay unconscious in a bedroom off the corridor, as comfortable as they could make her. Lying awkwardly, she looked like a strange worn-out puppet with her matted plait and lab coat the colour of dust. Ivan pulled out his mobile phone to call for an ambulance. The screen lit up, then flickered off before he could open the keypad to dial. Wilfred tried to make his perso-text work with similar lack of success.

"My phone's not working."

"My perso-text is flat... I think..."

Jess ran to the phone, a heavy black object like something from an old film. She dialled triple zero. "Hello? Hello? This is an emergency. Can you hear me? The stupid thing's not working."

Ivan stared at the UHF radio. A light flashed. He tried to remember how it worked, but the flickering light and the sound of Jess jiggling the receiver of the old phone, Wilfred turning the handle of his device, and Cassie saying, "Can you hear me?" over and over to the professor in the next room prevented coherent thought. Ivan's phone beeped, but the screen flashed on and off so quickly that he couldn't make it work.

"This is crazy," said Jess in the same agitated voice she'd used on the doorstep. "Someone turn that cursed light off. It's giving me a headache. Why doesn't anything work here?"

Ivan knew Jess only from his sister Reenie's description of her after their return from the other Willowvale last year. A tall, hard, spoilt girl, Reenie had said, who wanted Cassie's brother for herself. This edgy, scared girl in the most inappropriate outfit he'd ever seen out in the bush was nothing like Reenie's description, except for her height, exaggerated by ridiculously heeled satin shoes. In a weird way, she did look like Wilfred; something about the shape of the face and the way she moved her hands. But Ivan didn't have time to think about that now. His phone flashed on and he quickly dialled into it—but its screen blanked out before he finished dialling. He moved to the old landline phone, listening to the heavy earpiece that Jess had flung down. The dial tone pulsed on and off like a bee's wings as it landed and took off. Wilfred went to the window, still trying to make his perso-text function.

"What's wrong with it? I want to go home." Jess attacked the light switch, flicking it on and off, but without any effect on the lights' flashing.

"I think it's starting to charge." Wilfred had his device plugged into a cradle and cable near the phone.

Cassie filled a glass and took water to the professor. "She's stirring. Ivan, help. She needs water. She looks a little better."

Ivan went to see. He and Cassie knelt by the professor, holding a glass to her lips. Wilfred followed.

"Nobody cares about me getting home," said Jess loudly in the kitchen. "I can't stand it. I'm walking there." Ivan heard her stride across the kitchen, fling the door open and step out, slamming the door behind her.

Ivan's phone signalled an incoming text. "Oh, I've got coverage." The message, however, was a disconnected jumble of letters that meant nothing.

The professor stirred, struggled, coughed, and said indistinctly, "I can't do it any more."

"Professor!" said Ivan.

"I…can't…do…it…any…more." She lapsed back into unconsciousness.

"What can't she do any more?"

There was a vaguely musical sound from Wilfred's device in the kitchen. It whirred, clicked and fed out a long strip of paper tape. Wilfred went to investigate. "This is gobbeldegook. I can't read it. I wish Jess hadn't forgotten her perso-text, it's probably better than mine…"

Cassie went to see what Wilfred's device was doing. Ivan stayed, holding the professor's hand.

"Ivan, Wilfred, come and look at this," said Cassie from the kitchen.

Responding to something urgent in her voice, Ivan went to see.

"Look outside."

The strange flashing of the kitchen light was behind but it seemed to Ivan that it reflected on the window in a barely perceptible change about once a second. Yet it was brighter outside than in; how could there be a reflection?

"What, exactly, are we looking at?" asked Wilfred.

"It's changing. Every time the light flickers in here, something changes out there."

"This is doing my head in," said Ivan. He forced his eyes to stay on the hot light outside. At first, accustomed to the darker interior, all he could see was the white-blue sky and neutral coloured summer landscape.

"This is as weird as a flying wombat," said Wilfred.

"I can't see anything. The flashing light in here is distracting—"

"Can't you see it?"

"I'm trying to see. But the light bulb is interfering—"

"That's not the light bulb."

"I don't understand."

Cassie pointed outside. "Look. It changes. The actual sky changes."

Ivan screwed up his eyes to shut out the distractions of the room behind and pressed his nose against the smudged glass of the window. Cassie was right. Without the wavering electric light, there was still something oddly rhythmic happening outside; a regular subtle change like a page turning or a bird flying across the sun. Something that was difficult to pin down… something to be seen only out of the corner of your eye. He closed his eyes and opened them to see newly. The changes were quick and regular. "I see it changing," he said slowly. And it was. Like a jerky animation the line of trees across the small plateau on which the observatory stood was one moment the tall forest it should be. The next moment it was a ring of immature trees, olive green leaves tipped with red. The trees were quite different—and then as they had been—again and again.

"The trees. What are they doing?"

"Look at the sky."

In time with the trees, the sky, too, changed. From a dazzling hazy white to clear blue, and back, like a blink.

Cassie touched Ivan's shoulder. "See the smoke?"

A line of white a different shade from the sky appeared, disappeared, reappeared, vanished.

"What is that? I thought the bushfire fizzled out."

"Didn't you say that this place is the intersection between the two worlds?" Wilfred asked Ivan and Cassie.

"Yes."

"I think we're seeing both of them, one after the other, over and over."

Ivan looked back into the kitchen. The scene there pulsed to the same rhythm as the sky. "What does it mean?"

Wilfred stiffened. "Where's Jess?"

Nobody knew. "Oh yeah. She said something about going home," said Cassie.

"She's gone out there?" said Wilfred with panic creeping into his voice. Everyone turned to the window again. Now that Ivan knew what was happening, he couldn't ignore the disturbing pulse from one sky to the other, the jump of the trees. Jess was nowhere to be seen. "I have to go and find her," said Wilfred.

Ivan and Cassie grabbed him.

"Let me go!"

"No!"

Wilfred was stronger than Ivan expected. "You can't go outside. Who knows what could happen?"

"I have to find Jess."

"It might be dangerous."

There was a thump on the back porch, very like the thump of the professor falling in the hallway when they arrived. Wilfred broke away from Cassie and Ivan.

"Stop!" screamed Cassie so forcefully that Wilfred paused. "It's dangerous. Check the porch. Is she there?"

Wilfred, panting, peered through a small pane in the door. "I can see her foot. I have to get her. She's collapsed. She needs help. She's my sister."

Ivan said, "Look at her. She went outside. What if that happens to you too?"

Cassie, watching the sky carefully, said suddenly, "It's like skipping."

"Have you gone crazy?"

"Listen to me. It's like skipping. The rope's up, then the rope's down. That's when you jump. There's an opportunity you have to take at exactly the right instant. Get it right, you're fine. Look. The sky's here, the sky's there. I think if we get her in between changes, we'll all be okay; but we mustn't get it wrong."

"Really?"

"Look at Jess. Something happened to her. She probably just walked out there willy-nilly, at the wrong moment. That's why she's…hurt, or whatever."

The sky continued to pulse disturbingly.

"When I tell you, open the door and we'll pull her in." Cassie seemed very sure.

"How can you know?"

"Can you think of anything better? It won't hurt to do it that way, anyway. Have you ever skipped?"

"Yes, when I was in primary school," said Ivan.

"Then you should understand," said Cassie.

They clustered at the door. "Now!" Cassie flung the door open. Jess lay on the step. Ivan and Wilfred grabbed her by the arms and dragged her inside. Cassie slammed the door.

Jess lay with closed eyes, a strange paleness across her face and arms, breathing fast and shallow in time with the rhythm of the sky and the light bulb. They half lifted, half dragged her to a divan in the corner where the professor kept her easel and paints.

"Jess, wake up," Wilfred said over and over. He sat down on the floor next to the divan, holding her limp hand.

"This is fun," said Cassie, and sat down at the kitchen table.

Ivan had done a first aid course at school this term. He thought Jess was okay…well he didn't think she would die. She was pale and wouldn't wake up; she was breathing, at least. He felt her pulse. With a shock he realized that her pulse synchronized with the rhythm of the changes in the sky and the flashing of the light bulb—which was about the speed of a normal heartbeat. He went and sat at the table with Cassie.

"She's okay for now, but something weird is going on. It's as if she's in time with the sky and the lights. What do we do now?"

"I don't know. We're trapped here. If we go out, we could all end up like Jess. There's probably no way out of here at all," said Cassie dully.

"Don't be silly. We'll work it out."

There was a depressed silence.

"Jess was right. The light will give us all headaches," said Ivan, but he felt too tired to do anything about it. He put his arms on the table and laid his head on them.

CHAPTER FOURTEEN

OUTSIDE

When Ivan woke it was afternoon. The sun beat in through the window, across the sink, down to the floor and onto his back. Cassie slept on the other side of the table in the same position he'd found himself in. He stretched and saw that Wilfred was asleep, leaning against the divan. Jess was the same as before.

Feeling thirsty, Ivan fetched a cup of water, and thought he'd take one to the professor. Her bedroom faced west, the same as the kitchen, but a frayed black curtain shaded the window and the room was dark. "Professor, it's Ivan. Are you feeling better yet?" He felt his way across the room, his eyes unaccustomed to the dim light. His knee hit the bed and Ivan lurched forward, spilling the water.

The professor wasn't there.

Ivan flung the curtain open. The subtly pulsing light of the two skies flooded into the room. The bed was empty, sheets tangled. An old grey blanket lay rumpled on the floor. Ivan rushed into the corridor. It was empty. He opened the next door. Another bedroom, similar but disused, and as empty as the other. Its tattered curtain moved in the breeze from a smashed window. Surely the professor hadn't gone out that way.

The front door was closed. Ivan opened it. He blinked at the strange light outside. No sign of the professor out there. Remembering that the door was sprung to close and lock, he found a stone behind the door and used it as it had no doubt been used before to prop the door open.

"Ivan! Don't go out there!" Cassie was awake.

"The professor's gone."

"She can't have. She was unconscious."

"Take a look if you don't believe me."

Cassie went into the professor's room and came out almost immediately. "Where is she?"

Ivan gestured to the wide world. "No idea. I was just about to go and look for her."

"You idiot," said Cassie. She grabbed his arm.

"What?"

"Have you forgotten? D'you want to end up like Jess?"

He had forgotten. Ivan snatched his arm back. "Of course not. But we have to find the professor. She's old and sick, probably got dementia or something too."

"She can't have got far. Maybe she's gone to the observatory. Is there a way through to there from here?"

"Only outside, unless there's a secret tunnel. And they're only in stories."

They stared out at the strange flickering landscape. From this side of the building the differences in the hills were barely noticeable, but the two motorbikes appeared and disappeared constantly from view in a disturbing manner. The shadow of the house extended across the bare dusty area outside, the same all the time.

"What do we do?" said Ivan, partly to himself.

Cassie grabbed his arm again, and pointed. "Look!"

"What?"

"I can see footprints."

Ivan couldn't see any.

"You can only see them in one of the worlds. The one without the motorbikes. She must have gone out into just that world, Ivan. Between the flashes, like I thought…"

"So if we want to find her at all, we have to get into that world too."

"She's probably gone to the observatory. Do you think if we're careful we could get out into that world?"

"I don't know. It's a big risk. What if she's not there? Then what do we do?"

"How about we take a few things in case we have to go further? We'll have to work out how to get back into this house whatever we do."

Leaving the door propped open they returned to the kitchen. Wilfred and Jess were sleeping as before. Cassie rummaged in cupboards and found a metal water bottle. Ivan found some dried-up apples and plain biscuits. They searched for a map, but found none. Ivan tried the phone again, but it crackled in and out of service. Cassie pulled an ancient canvas backpack from a top cupboard.

Wilfred woke. "What's going on?" he asked fuzzily.

"The professor's missing. We have to go and look for her."

Wilfred jumped up. "I'll come too."

There was a pause.

"What about Jess?"

Another pause.

"Someone has to stay with her."

Wilfred looked from Ivan and Cassie to the sleeping Jess, and slumped. "Good old Wilfred. Responsible, reliable Wilfred," he said.

"We won't be long. She can't have gone far. If Jess is your sister, like you said…" Cassie began.

"Yeah. All that. Of course I'm the one to stay." Wilfred sat heavily on a stool next to the phones and radio.

"We'll be as quick as we can."

"Yeah, I know, I know. But just once—" Wilfred put his hands over his face in a weary gesture. "I'd like to be—" he stopped speaking.

"Be what, Wilfred?" asked Cassie. Ivan felt very uncomfortable.

"The one you want to be with," Wilfred blurted out.

Ivan had known this was coming. Dreaded it. He realized he was holding his breath.

"Wilfred…" said Cassie, who looked stricken too.

"You don't have to explain," said Wilfred.

Ivan wished that Jess was awake and would say something tactless to break the tension.

"You must know that you're one of my best friends."

"Yeah. Best-friends-just-good-friends…there's nothing *just* about it. That was a bad pun." Wilfred blushed. Ivan was not sure if this was because he was embarrassed at the pun, or whether it was because of the confrontation.

Ivan knew he was part of this tangle but he couldn't make himself speak. He knew exactly how Wilfred felt, he thought…but…well, he also knew he, Ivan, had kissed Cassie, and hadn't been rejected. His breath caught in his throat as he remembered. It was all too much in the middle of everything else. He found himself melting away from Cassie and Wilfred.

"What do *you* want, Cassie?" said Wilfred, pointlessly.

"I can't magically make everyone happy. It's impossible." Cassie looked uncharacteristically as if she would cry.

"She should let us fight it out," said Wilfred angrily in Ivan's vague direction. "I'd win easily."

"Don't be stupid, Wilfred. I'm not a prize. It doesn't work like that."

Once before, Ivan had clashed physically with Wilfred, and it was an experience he did not want to repeat. His palms started to sweat.

Cassie looked as if she really was going to cry; but she didn't. She put her hand on Wilfred's arm. "Can we discuss this later?"

Wilfred looked at her hand as if it were an object he didn't recognize. He looked sad.

"What difference will that make? None at all."

In the pause that followed, a stretched-out moment that seemed to drag on forever, Ivan heard Jess' quick, shallow breathing change. The irritating flick of the lights changed too. Outside the shift between the two skies still synchronized with the lights.

The door closed behind them with a clang. The two motorbikes were nowhere to be seen. The sky was a hot, hazy white. The faint footprints of the professor crossed the fine dust of the driveway in the direction of the observatory. Ivan and Cassie were in Ivan's version of the world. The fact that the sky and landscape no longer changed from one world to the other was calming, but Ivan's heart still raced after getting out of the professor's house, afraid of choosing the wrong moment and ending up like Jess, pulsing with every switch.

"We did it," said Cassie.

Ivan felt tired. We could just go home, he thought. Wilfred and Jess will work out how to get back to their world. He blushed at his own horribleness. What was he thinking? It must be a reaction to that awkward conflict with Wilfred. How could he? Wilfred had helped him more than once. Jess was an unknown quantity; but they couldn't abandon her.

The observatory door was open. Cassie called out, "Professor?" There was no answer, and not a sound inside. They entered and found themselves in a small office with a desk piled with faded folders and box files. A metal cupboard stood against the wall, and a large incomprehensible chart on a noticeboard was dotted with rusty drawing pins connected by a spider's web of sewing cotton. Items that Ivan and Cassie could not identify lay on every flat surface. There was no way the professor could be hidden in here. They checked in the cupboard to make sure, but it was full of electrical panels with complicated wiring and black dials marked with mysterious acronyms and strange abbreviated words.

Dust lay everywhere except for a pathway between the door, the desk and another open door which led into the telescope room. The domed roof was closed. It was dark and shadowy but for the flashing of a red light on a monitor. Ivan found the light switch and turned on the lights.

"Professor? Are you here?" It took only a minute to search the room. There was no sign of the professor. The only thing out of place in the scientific tidiness was an open metal cupboard. Inside was an old electrical switchboard with many exposed coloured wires. Below, a deep, empty shelf. Ivan read the plastic label. It read, simply, *Scope*.

"This is the only thing missing," he said.

"She obviously isn't here."

"I guess we'll have to go out and look for her."

They went to the top of a small rocky peak at the edge of the plateau on which the observatory was situated to survey the land and try to work out what to do.

After some discussion they agreed to head north. The south contained the roads they'd come by. The south-west led to outlying farms in the Willowvale area. To the east was the almost impenetrable mountainous country where long ago Raven and Thistle had been lost. It was to the north and northwest that they agreed was the direction to go, toward the lines of hills that disappeared to the horizon, mysterious as fog. The line of hills from which the faint line of smoke now rose. If the odd Professor Fenella Carter had wandered anywhere, they thought, it would be in that direction.

They set out across the open tableland. Leaving the lookout peak they entered a burnt forest, uneasily silent. The land ahead looked as confusing as a cloth thrown over a pile of junk.

A smell of fire enveloped them. Their feet crunched on blackened grass. It was strangely quiet; the birds had moved away although the fire had been light and burnt only grasses and low plants. Leaves rattled eerily with slight movements of air. Footsteps sounded unusually loud. Cassie and Ivan did not speak, unnerved by the scene. Threads of smoke rose here and there. Trees untouched by the fire made patches of green shade like puddles. The ground fell away steeply from the plateau, littered with boulders. At the bottom of the slope that marked its edge a small creek trickled, vegetation at its edges completely untouched. They stopped.

"It's lucky we found this creek. We didn't bring much water."

They stooped to drink from the creek then rested on the warm stones of its bank.

"There's something odd going on."

"Lots of odd things. Like that the fire has gone out—"

"Why did the professor wander away?"

Shadows fell across them in stripes. Ivan looked up at through the burnt leaves to the bright sky and remembered that it was Saturday afternoon because it had only been this morning that he looked through leaves at the sky in the same way.

"This is a wild goose chase," said Cassie. "How do we know that the professor isn't hiding round the back of the house, or in the outhouse, or behind a tree? We should have looked harder. She seemed pretty crazy to me. I've only met her once and heard about her from Thistle and Raven. Maybe she's…I don't know. Not to be trusted."

"I know what you mean. She wears black glasses and says she's blind… but also says she's an astronomer and an artist," said Ivan.

"The way she talks, sometimes sharp as a tack then suddenly dotty as a quoll. How do we know if that's real, or whether she wants us to think she's a bit crazy for some reason of her own? How old is she? If she's out there and if she is blind, and old, then she can't have got far. She'll be having trouble…but if she's up to something we could be in big trouble ourselves." Cassie picked up a stick and drew a rough map on the ground. "It's like looking for a needle in a hundred haystacks," she said.

"I'm worried about Wilfred and Jess too. How are they going to get home if Jess is so sick? It wasn't easy for us to get out of the building in one piece."

"In one world, you mean," said Cassie.

"It seems that the connection between the two worlds is somehow dependent on the professor. So, we have to take the chance that Wilfred and Jess will be okay. We don't have much choice."

Cassie scribbled over her map with angry strokes of the stick. "Not much choice is right. The choice of wandering around these hills not knowing anything about why the professor is missing or where she might be…or not looking for her which almost certainly means losing any chance of moving between the worlds again. The choice of trying and failing and maybe being responsible for something bad happening to Jess and Wilfred or the choice of…" she flung the stick into the creek. "The choices are all bad. There's no way we can get anything right."

There was a disconsolate silence.

A frog called in the creek. Far away a cockatoo shrieked its harsh cry. A thump down the gully betrayed the presence of a wallaby and a breath of wind moved the leaves above them. Ivan sat, not focussed on anything particular, eyes directed to the silent hills.

CHAPTER FIFTEEN
IN THE BUSH

Cassie continued to talk about the unlikeliness of everything, but Ivan didn't hear. As he sat there, not only the landscape but the situation began to make a backwards kind of sense to him. He saw things that had not been visible to him a few minutes before. It was like suddenly being able to read, or to understand a code. A kangaroo or wallaby trail like the ones he'd followed in the bush near home on Friday morning came into focus. It had previously been part of the chaos of the bush, but now it resolved into meaning. He went to investigate.

The feeling of being inside a story came over Ivan like a wave breaking. Why resist? He didn't want to get lost, so he collected small pieces of white quartz and placed them as he walked to mark his route, like Hansel and Gretel. He'd only gone a hundred metres when there were shouts and footsteps. Cassie caught up with him.

"Ivan, what are you doing? We have to work together. Nice trail marking, by the way. But we have to stick together."

"I think this is the way we have to go to find the professor."

"What about all the things we talked about? She could be anywhere. We have to plan."

"We can't sit around talking about it. We have to *do* something."

"But how can we know we're doing the right thing? And what about all those other risks?"

"I thought you were the impulsive one," replied Ivan.

Cassie stamped. "I am! But it's all so big, and there really are a lot of dangers. And how can we be sure that this is the way to go?"

"I've got a feeling."

"A feeling isn't good enough, Ivan. We've got to do this logically."

"But don't you see? Logic isn't going to get us anywhere. The only thing logic reliably tells us is that the professor can't have got far because she's old and probably blind. Put that together with my…feeling, if that's what we call it. The odds are better already."

"A feeling can't compete with logic. Anything could happen."

"Yeah, but—"

"I think it's urgent that we find Professor Carter, even if the only reason is that she's an old lady, possibly blind and confused."

"Yes. So let's follow this trail and my hunch. It's a good plan."

"Hmph. I wouldn't go that far."

"Got any better ideas?"

"No."

Ivan and Cassie were halfway up the next ridge, still following the wallaby trail and Ivan's hunch. The trail of small quartz pieces glittered like a line of buttons down the hill. "I never thought of Hansel and Gretel as a useful story before," Cassie said.

"I hope there's no scary witch in a gingerbread house at the end of this story."

The trail led to the top of the ridge then petered out. Low vegetation was singed but not seriously burnt. They climbed to the top of an outcrop of rocks to see what lay beyond. Another very complex valley entered by many steep gullies lay precipitously below; beyond were more ridges and valleys, equally confusing. The range of hills resembled a maze.

The fire had been in this new valley, leaving stark black bark and bare ground at the base of tree trunks. There were no signs of flames or embers now; however, a thread of smoke rose from a deep gully, changing colour as it crossed from shade to sunshine, dispersing as it reached the altitude of the ridge. This further land was even less inviting than the valley from which Ivan and Cassie had climbed.

They looked back. Far below the creek glittered, and past it was the open meadow with the lookout peak, and the small geometric blocks that were the observatory. Beyond this, the wooded hills and cleared land out of Willowvale faded to opal colours.

Ivan thought, *I don't know what to do. This area looks like the sort of place where getting lost is more likely than not. We might not ever be found.* He wondered whether this was all a bad dream, except for the good bits like seeing Cassie and Wilfred again. "Maybe we should go back—"

"No. We've come this far. I think you might be right. The professor is in danger, and she is probably the key to the link between the worlds. We have to find her. This is the most likely direction."

"But how?" Ivan slid down the boulder and landed in a thorny bush at its base, getting a long scratch down his arm. "Ow. Why do I always hurt myself?" His confidence in his hunch about finding Professor Carter deflated.

Cassie slid down after him and took Ivan's hand. "Show me. You'll live. I'll kiss it better. There."

"Stop it. I'm not a baby." Ivan snatched his hand away and hung his head. "Cassie, I was wrong."

Cassie opened her mouth to reply, but Ivan interrupted.

"Look!"

"What?"

On the ground next to the boulder was a footprint on the fire-dried ground. Ivan was too excited to speak.

Cassie crouched down to inspect it. "That's not my footprint or yours. It's the same as the ones the professor left on the driveway. Going that way," she pointed down the valley.

"I guess this means we have to go down there."

Cassie nodded. They took note of the area, planted a larger piece of quartz and made an arrow of sticks to lead them back into the wallaby trail, filled their pockets with more quartz pebbles and set off down the hill.

Ivan had read about tracking in the bush and how much information could be discovered from looking at marks on the ground. It wasn't that easy. He couldn't tell that the footprints were made by a woman, 161 centimetres tall, weighing 64 kilos, wearing size 38 shoes worn on the outside of the heels. All he saw were footprints travelling off the crest of the ridge and down. He and Cassie followed them. There was no other person here. The footprints had to have been made by the professor.

They reached a creek at the bottom of the second valley. The tracks showed that the professor had stopped here and scouted up and down for a place to cross.

"This is very confusing. Where can she have gone from here?"

"And why? The trail looks very purposeful."

They had a drink from the creek.

"Surely we'll catch up with her soon. She can't be more than a few minutes ahead of us."

Eventually they found the place where the professor had crossed the creek. Her tracks pointed confidently onto another kangaroo trail that climbed out of the gully. The afternoon was still hot but shadows lengthened exaggeratedly down the steep slope. By the time they reached the top of the next ridge, they could see the end of the afternoon racing toward them from the west. The professor's tracks continued down the other side of the ridge. Ivan and Cassie followed wearily, slipping on the steep slope. How could the professor have done it? This time her trail traversed the hill diagonally, skirted the head of a small creek and climbed again. Soon Ivan and Cassie were on the edge of a knife-like ridge that divided two gullies. They looked around the corner of the ridge into a gully so steeply enclosed that it became a gorge.

"It's like another world," exclaimed Cassie.

It was true. The bush here, sheltered from the sun and untouched by the fire, was of tall alpine ash trees under-frilled with tree ferns and flowering shrubs. The professor's tracks crossed the ridge and disappeared into thick undergrowth.

"I think we're getting close," said Ivan.

"A feeling?"

"No." Ivan pointed. Deep in the gorge was the source of the thread of smoke.

It was much more difficult to move through this enclosed gorge than it had been to cross the more open ridges with their thinner, burnt out undergrowth. Cassie had the feeling that she should have been leading the way, but it was Ivan's quest, and she knew what it was to be on a quest.

They shoved their way through, no longer looking for footprints. Now and then there was sight of the thread of smoke that rose from deep in the gorge. They traversed the steep valley wall, slipping in leaf mould and hanging onto branches to stop themselves from sliding down the slope. Every bird that had fled from the fire must have come here; the air was full of their calls. It was dim and cool and green. Something moved ahead of them. Cassie saw a scaly tail flick into the leaves. She didn't say anything to Ivan, who had stepped over that place a moment before. No point frightening him.

A creek bed full of jumbled boulders and tiny dry waterfalls lay below them. The column of white smoke loomed up into the sky like a faint tree trunk.

Ivan disappeared into the bushes.

"Where are you?" called Cassie, feeling scared for the first time. "Cooee?" She stopped to listen for Ivan's reply. There was no reply. "Ivan? Where are you? Cooee!" she called again, and listened. There was crashing in the bushes ahead, but no answer from Ivan; more rustling and crashing, and Cassie saw leaves at the top of bushes ahead move in concert with someone…something…moving below. Was that Ivan, or Professor Carter, or some large creature? Cassie's heart beat faster than ever. The movement in the leaves shifted up the valley. Why didn't Ivan answer?

Taking a deep breath and a sighting of the pale column of smoke ahead, Cassie made a decision and plunged into the bushes in the direction of the smoke and the movement. "I hope this is a good idea," she thought as she pushed through bushes, trying not to think about ticks and spiders and the snake she'd seen. Bursting through a wall of leaves, she found herself in a small clearing. A large tree, split down its trunk and burnt by lightning stood next to a hole in the ground that could have been the entrance to an old mine, or a limestone sinkhole, or perhaps just a hole.

"Ivan!" she yelled as she brushed the last leaves off her face. Her voice echoed down from the rocky sides of the gorge and up from the hole. There was no answer. Cassie warily moved closer to the edge and peered down. To her surprise the hole was half filled with water which flowed in from the gorge above. Smoke rose from the ruined tree into the still air.

Across the hole Cassie saw two people. One was Ivan; the other a slightly stooped figure in grey with a long fuzzy plait. They were bent over something at the edge of the water.

"Ivan!" called Cassie again, angrily. Why had he not answered before? She scrambled over rocks and dirt, around the edge of the hole. When she was a few metres away, panting over shifting stones, Ivan and the professor turned toward her.

Ivan smiled. "There you are," he said.

The professor's ambiguous face followed Cassie's progress as she approached. "I've been showing Ivan," she said.

Cassie was confused. She did not understand what was going on. She came up to the others. The professor held out her hand as if she wanted to shake hands, and Cassie did so.

"Which of your friends is this?"

"Cassie."

"Ah, we've met," said the professor.

"We'd better start back to the observatory, it's going to be dark before long," Cassie said. She put her hand on Ivan's arm. "We have to go. The others will be worried."

"In good time, Cassie," said the professor. "I need to take more readings."

Cassie saw that the object at their feet was a device with dials and blinking lights; some kind of scientific meter that lay at the edge of the hole. A cable coiled from the metal box that was the outer part of the machine into the water. Beeps and clicks sounded. Numbers and a graph moved across a screen.

Ivan drew Cassie a little away and whispered in her ear, "I've been trying to get her to come."

"I can hear you," said the professor.

"We have to get back," Cassie whispered to Ivan. "I'm worried about Wilfred…and Jess. I think Thistle and Raven will worry about me. I don't know what the professor is up to. Everything is wrong. We have to sort it out."

"Stop that whispering," said the professor. "This is…this is…" her voice faltered. She swayed. Cassie, thinking she was about to faint, lunged toward her. The sky flickered. Perhaps a large bird passed overhead, Cassie thought. The professor recovered before Cassie reached her. Cassie closed her eyes. She imagined returning to the observatory, and that everything had turned out fine, that she would catch up with Pip and that life would be happy and explained.

"Cassie? Are you okay?" She felt Ivan's arm around her shoulders. He was looking into her face in concern, she knew. She drew in a slow breath and opened her eyes. Ivan put both arms around her and held her for a long time. She heard the professor mutter, "A bit of peace at last," and heard the beeps and clicks of the apparatus, a trickle of water falling into the pool and birds calling in the gorge. Past Ivan's shoulder, Cassie saw the professor folding her machine into a case.

"Seeing as you two have bothered to chase me all the way out here, you can carry the terraspectromultiscope back." She stood waiting for them to reply. Cassie took Ivan's hand and whispered to him, "Is she really blind?"

"I don't know."

"I heard that. Come along, it's getting late. I've got work to do."

A full moon rose as they reached the knife-edged ridge that marked the boundary of the gorge. The professor held onto Cassie's arm; Ivan carried the machine in its case inside an old canvas bag. Professor Carter became vague and confused. It was difficult to imagine that she could see much, if anything now. Cassie wanted to ask many questions, but it took all her concentration to help the professor through the bush.

Moonlight shone on the white stones that marked their route. After a while the unearthly light, and the flash of white that was the trail of quartz had a hypnotic effect. Cassie felt disconnected and disoriented. The white marker stones became more and more difficult to spot.

They stopped to let the professor rest. She was panting and did not speak, looking about her in a puzzled, almost panic-stricken way. A cloud moved briefly across the moon, or perhaps a nightbird flew. Cassie, arm released, scouted ahead to find the trail. The next white marker lay on the ground in the direction the ones before had indicated. Ivan looked down. "That's weird," he said, and pointed at a stone further along that was a faint outline in the moonlight. They walked on, expecting to see another, but there were none. "I'm sure I started marking the trail before here," said Ivan.

"It's confusing. I can't tell where we are."

The professor leaned on a tree trunk with her head against the bark and said nothing.

Cassie and Ivan stared at the surrounding forest and the side of the hill with increasing incomprehension and unease.

"It's lucky we're nearly back at the first creek. We can't possibly be lost.

Even if we're off the route you marked we'll be able to find our way."

"It doesn't make sense. Look around."

Cassie looked. "I can look around until I'm dizzy, but it doesn't make sense. Where are the stones you marked the trail with?"

"The creek's down there, and we're on the kangaroo trail so the observatory must be across—but look."

"What?" Cassie began to lose her temper. "Stop telling me to look."

"The trees."

"What about them?"

"They're not burnt. They should be burnt."

He was right. Cassie whirled around, careless of dizziness. Trees in every direction, shadowy in the moonlight but definitely not burnt. The smell of grass, eucalyptus and pollen, but nothing of fire. "I don't understand."

"We must be a lot further off the trail than we thought," said Ivan in a worried voice.

The professor cleared her throat. "Follow me."

In every respect except for the burntness of the bush, and the disappearance of the white stones, the route seemed correct. Cassie was so confused that she couldn't even try to work out what was going on. She took Professor Carter's arm to help her along, but in an odd way felt as if she drew strength from the older woman rather than the other way around. Ivan swapped the professor's bag to his other hand and followed.

The professor guided them down to the creek that should have been the one they remembered, and up the slope opposite. The hills rose, hiding the moon, and deeper darkness fell. After a long time, they reached the crest of the slope and flatter ground near the observatory. The area was open and a dome of stars stretched above the fallen forest and regrown trees that ringed the meadow.

Cassie and Ivan stopped.

"What's wrong?" asked Professor Carter. "We're nearly there."

"Where are we?"

"Almost there," repeated the professor.

"But it's all different."

"I don't know what you're talking about. Everything is the same."

"But…but…" Ivan's voice was puzzled. "We found you in my world—this is the other one."

"Of course you didn't. I've been in this world all the time. You children are confused. Your friends will be waiting for you. You can all go home."

"They're at the observatory all right, they're stuck there. Jess is sick."

"Stuff and nonsense. She can't be. It's not a place to be sick." The professor gripped Cassie's arm tightly. "I don't need to tell him to send them back. He knows how dangerous it is for them." She tugged at Cassie's arm to hurry her up. "We've got to get back there and sort this out. I've got important work to do." She started walking quite briskly toward the observatory, which could be seen as a dim silhouette against the sky.

Ivan picked up the case of scientific equipment.

Cassie felt irritated. The professor hurried now, dragging her along. She was annoying. Wandering off, getting lost in that precipitous, dangerous valley, expecting Wilfred and Jess to sort themselves out. What was her pointless, mysterious mission? Who was she talking about, to "send them back"? As they approached the observatory, Cassie saw with relief that there was a light in the kitchen window. They crossed the tableland on a kangaroo trail—or perhaps one made by humans—that picked its way between obstacles. Around the meadow, fallen old trees and spindly young ones distorted in the night to wild and threatening shapes. "Did you bring a torch?"

The professor laughed. "What use would a torch be to me?"

"I don't believe you're really blind," Cassie said without thinking.

The professor stopped and turned to face Cassie, the black lenses of her glasses reflecting the stars. "It's not your business to doubt me, nor to judge what you don't know. It's not wise." She started walking again, so suddenly that Cassie, supporting the professor's arm, nearly overbalanced, almost causing them to fall. The professor continued to hurry toward the observatory, but her pace slowed steadily and soon her reliance on Cassie's arm was considerable. The kitchen light glowed welcomingly as they reached the back porch.

"I will need your help to analyse my data," said the professor faintly, as with difficulty Cassie helped her up the steps. The professor's words faded to nothing and she collapsed on the porch, in exactly the same spot where Jess had fallen.

CHAPTER SIXTEEN
WAITING

Wilfred stood at the kitchen window. He saw Ivan and Cassie start out across the plateau, flicking out of view and back as the two worlds switched. It was like watching an ancient movie on a stuttering projector. As far as he could tell, Cassie and Ivan were walking in Ivan's world. They didn't turn back to wave. He sighed. He'd known all along that no matter how fond Cassie was of him, she'd choose Ivan when it came down to it. He'd tried to be realistic, but now realized that secret hopes are difficult to destroy without the intervention of reality, no matter how much logic one tries to use on oneself.

The flip between the two worlds seemed to be slower, and though it was wildly strange, it became slightly less disturbing to watch. The change came every couple of seconds now. He was glad they'd got out in one piece, and the thought reminded him of Jess.

His sister. He was still getting used to the idea of having a sibling, which was something he'd secretly wished for all his life. Though the last (was it only twenty-four?) hours had been tumultuous, he was pretty happy to have Jess. Despite her faults, he already felt the same loyalty to her that he felt toward his mother. Rex, on the other hand, the embodiment of his mythical father, was a disappointment so intense that Wilfred put him out of his mind.

Jess stirred, opened her eyes and sat up dizzily. There was a flash from the light fitting. "What happened?" She looked around in a bemused fashion. "Where am I?" She put her hand to her forehead as if she really did have the headache that she'd threatened earlier.

Oh no. Had Jess lost her memory on top of everything?

Wilfred decided to act normally and hope that Jess would too. "We're at the old observatory. You went outside and fainted. You've been asleep for hours."

Jess looked puzzled and again Wilfred wondered whether she'd suffered some form of amnesia; but she said, "Where are the others?"

"They've—"

"I wanted to go home. I still do. To Willowvale. I was going to walk."

"It's too late now."

Jess looked alarmed. "What do you mean, too late?"

"Only that it's late. In the day."

Jess dropped the topic of Willowvale, Wilfred suspected only temporarily, and said again, "Where are the others? Cassie and that Ivan boy?"

"They've gone to look for the professor."

Wilfred could almost see Jess' memories of the afternoon flowing back into her mind one at a time.

"And the old woman who lives here?"

Wilfred explained to the best of his ability.

Jess was silently attentive while he spoke. "The old woman won't go far," she said. "Why are we hanging around here?"

"Do you know what happened to you when you went outside? Why you got sick? You still don't look a hundred percent."

Jess said thoughtfully, "I went out. I was going to walk to Willowvale, but it was horrible out there. I felt as if I was being pulled through a keyhole and back, every second. I couldn't walk home. I couldn't even walk around to the front door. I tried but I couldn't. It was like walking with a boulder tied to each foot. I decided to go back inside. That's all I remember until now."

Wilfred sat next to Jess on the divan.

"So are we trapped here?" asked Jess.

"Yes. And no."

"What the blinking frogmouth does that mean?" said Jess. Wilfred was relieved that she was back to normal.

"Cassie and Ivan did get out in one piece. But we have to wait until they get back."

"Why?" asked Jess rhetorically, then answering her own question: "Too clueless to get home without us. So this weird professor had a miraculous recovery."

"While we were all worried about you, she disappeared. She's old and sick. She wandered off."

"Yeah, yeah. But why are you all so fixated on her? Who is she? Just a crazy deluded person who thinks she's a scientist."

"She might be all that, but she's still a person."

Jess changed the subject again. "I don't understand. What is this place? What's going on? Why can't I go outside without nearly dying?"

Wilfred knew little more than Jess did about these questions. He also realized with a shock that Jess knew nothing of the other world, the one Ivan came from. In all the turmoil of the past day and night many things had happened, and many things had been forgotten. The moment he tried to explain to Jess, would she assume he was crazier than the professor? He had to explain despite this risk, but where to start? The beginning? Too complicated. The end? No idea what that would be. He'd have to explain from the middle, where they were right now.

Outside, the two skies continued to swap in regular time. He drew in a slow breath and pointed out the window. "See the sky, how it keeps changing?"

"I don't like it. I'm not looking at it."

Wilfred struggled to explain. "Can you try to look just for a few seconds? It's the only way I can explain. If the sky bothers you too much, look at the trees."

"I'm not interested in trees…oh." Jess stopped speaking and ran from the kitchen window to the pane in the back door to the professor's room, looking at the scene from each. "Maybe I'm getting a migraine or something." She went to the front door and opened it enough to see outside. Suddenly she drew her head back and slammed the door. "No."

"What?"

"You haven't explained anything to me yet."

"What did you see?"

Jess gestured to Wilfred to look for himself. He saw the hills and sky changing subtly. Movement in his peripheral vision caught his attention. He saw the two motorbikes, then none. Motorbikes. Empty ground. Bikes. No bikes.

"What is it? What does it mean?" Jess demanded.

"You see how there are different skies, and different trees, and now… disappearing bikes. It's another world. That's where Ivan comes from. The other world." Wilfred felt scared, witnessing this very clear demonstration of the parallel worlds. It was something he hadn't seen, any more than Jess had.

"That place where the sky is different and there are no motorbikes is where Ivan comes from?" Jess repeated dazedly. "Another world? Are you sure?"

"I can't explain it," said Wilfred.

"Can we get into it? Not that I want to."

"I don't know. Maybe. Ivan's got into this world more than once."

"Where, exactly, are Cassie and Ivan? And why is Ivan here, if he's from that other place? How did he get here?"

"I think Ivan and Cassie are in his world. Cassie and Ivan think this place is the door between the worlds."

"Why is Cassie here? Why was she wandering about in the bush when we met her?"

Wilfred didn't mean to tell Jess, but the words came out. "She's looking for her brother, Pip." He knew Jess and Pip had been friends, and that she had wanted to be more.

"Where is he?" Jess asked eagerly, then cut the question off short.

"He went into Ivan's world."

"Why? Why why why whywhywhy?" Jess repeated the word as if its meaning was wearing off, and she just wanted to make the sound.

"Um, he's in love with Ivan's sister."

Jess was silent for a moment then said, "I saw her once. A stranger. That's who that strange girl was, wearing his woolly hat. She was in Willowvale the night Pip came back. I saw her. She was with him then." They were back in the kitchen. Jess sat down at the table with a thud. "So what do we do now?"

"I don't know. We have to wait, I guess. Cassie, Ivan…and I think the professor's something to do with the link between our world…" said Wilfred, changing the subject.

"The real world."

"…and Ivan's world."

Jess stood up unsteadily and went to the window again. She looked out for a while, then left the room. Wilfred followed her. Once more she inspected the view from each window in the house. Ignoring Wilfred, she returned to the kitchen and stood at the window there, tapping a rhythm on the sink. "Have you been to this other world that Ivan is meant to have come from?"

"No."

"Do you think it's real? Does it actually exist? Maybe we're hallucinating or having mass hysteria or someone's drugged us."

That stopped Wilfred in his tracks. Jess' doubt seeped into him for a moment. "I haven't been there, but I saw Ivan and Reenie go back there last year. One second they were right in front of me, then they were gone, back to their world. And Cassie saw her brother go into Ivan's world a few days ago. The same."

Jess lost interest again. The shock she'd experienced outside seemed to have affected her attention span. "I'm hungry." They found tins of baked beans in the cupboard and ate them cold. "That professor could learn a thing or two about cooking," said Jess. "Mother is a great cook."

"Yeah, she is," said Wilfred, then shut up, remembering that Jess was not thinking of Berenice but of her stepmother.

"Let's look around while we're here. That old prof might have some interesting stuff. Let's look at the telescope. I've always wanted to see one."

"We'd have to go outside," said Wilfred doubtfully.

"Cassie and Ivan went outside. If they can, so can we. How did they do it?"

"Cassie has a theory that it's like jumping a skipping rope. You have to go at the right moment. If you do it wrong you get…tangled up. That's what happened to you before."

"And they got out okay?"

"I saw them walking across the meadow. They were fine."

"Let's do it. I want to see the telescope."

They stood at the front door for some time, watching the worlds flick one to the other.

"Which world shall we go into?"

"The real one, of course."

They propped the door open with a stone and poised themselves on the doorstep, ready to jump. Wilfred felt silly. Jess closed her eyes and took a deep breath in readiness. The moment stretched out for long seconds.

"Jess." Wilfred prodded her in the ribs. "Are you holding your breath?"

"What?"

"Do it again. Keep your eyes open."

"You're as nutty as a bogong near a lamp," remarked Jess. She did as Wilfred said.

Wilfred and Jess stared at each other. The peaceful afternoon with the clear sky and two motorcycles in the shadow of the house remained in front of them. Wilfred glanced down the hall and saw that the kitchen light shone a calm steady glow weak in the daylight.

Jess let her breath out. "Flying fruit bats." The scene suddenly switched, the light flickered, and the two landscapes alternated as before. "What was that?"

"Jess. Do it again."

This time the other landscape stayed in front of them, a hazy whitish sky and no bikes; but identical in every other respect.

"Am I controlling this somehow?" Jess grabbed Wilfred by the shoulders and shook him. The landscapes shook back and forth.

"Stop!"

"Sorry." Jess held her breath once more and jumped outside, pulling Wilfred with her. They landed in a heap on the dusty driveway, next to the parked bikes. Jess grabbed Wilfred and hugged him. "We did it!"

Wilfred hoped they'd be able to get back into the house.

"We could just go home, like we were going to last night, but I want to see the telescope first," said Jess. She jumped up, pulled Wilfred to his feet and dragged him by the hand toward the observatory building. Without her preposterous shoes she was the same height as him. With her elaborate hairstyle worn off and her excitement at seeing the telescope, Wilfred had a fleeting picture of the child Jess, who he hadn't known.

CHAPTER SEVENTEEN
INSIDE THE OBSERVATORY

Jess and Wilfred crossed the driveway to the observatory. The door was ajar. Inside, they found themselves in a windowless office lit only by daylight from the open door. It looked to Jess as if it had not been substantially changed for some years, and at the same time was in regular use.

In a corner of the office, partitions screened off a tiny area guarded by an engraved plastic sign saying *Staff Only*. Jess, curious, went in. Wilfred squeezed in behind her. Neatly pinned up inside the partitioned area were old photos and cuttings from newspapers. Jess' eye was caught by the word "Willowvale":

> **WILLOWVALE MYSTERY. The town of Willowvale is thought to have been damaged beyond hope by the force of the disaster last month, along with the complete destruction of the villages of Walgalu and Stirling. Communications and roads did not survive the impact. Rescue efforts will not be attempted due to continuing risk and security concerns.**

A fuzzy photograph showed a road sign saying *Walagu 10 km, Petrol, Hot Meals, Accommodation* behind a man (or woman, it was impossible to tell) in a full safety suit, looking like an astronaut from before the Disaster, complete with masked helmet and gloves. A stormy sky filled with smoke or ash glowered above. Below, on the same piece of newspaper, was a photo of a public notice inside a bold border:

WARNING
Do NOT enter the disaster zone.
Persons found entering the zone south of this point

WILL BE PROSECUTED.
DANGER
RISK OF CONTAMINATION
Fire risk continues.
Possible radiation.
Authorized personnel only to enter this zone.
Do NOT attempt to travel into the exclusion zone.
PENALTIES APPLY

The notice concluded with a reference for enquiries to: *Federal Government. State Government. Department of Defence. Fire Authority. Police.* And ended with insincere politeness: *We regret the inconvenience.*

Around this cutting, faded photos of people and houses were pinned. It looked like a quiet memorial for lost friends and relatives.

Feeling somehow sad, although she had experienced nothing of life before the Disaster nor knew of any family members who had perished in it, Jess left this strangely haunting shrine, with Wilfred on her heels. They went through a doorway that led further into the observatory. It was darker in there. Sculptural shapes of telescope equipment loomed in the dimness. On the far side of the room Jess saw a faint reflection from dials which caught the light like eyes. She found a switch, and the room was suddenly illuminated by lights shaded with deep metal covers that were placed around the walls like figures on a clock. Overcome with excitement she couldn't recall since she was a very small child, she ran to the eyepiece of the telescope and looked in.

Wilfred snorted slightly; he was suppressing a laugh. Jess laughed too. "It's day time. The roof isn't open. All I can see is blackness." She turned her attention to equipment ranged neatly round the walls. She understood none of it. Wilfred stood near the door, looking up at the inside of the domed roof. It was painted a deep blackish blue, decorated with golden stars arranged in constellations.

"I wonder who painted this, and why."

"For situations like this," Jess replied. "I'll come back when it's dark, and work out how to open the dome roof."

"The professor might show you, when they find her," Wilfred said.

"No, she won't." She left the telescope crouching splendidly in the centre of the room and made a circuit of the equipment at the perimeter of the space. None of it made sense to her.

"Jess."

"Yes?"

"Have you noticed? The lights. They're not flashing."

"Of course not. We're only here. Not here and there. The house is in both worlds…if they exist. The observatory is not. It's probably different in the other world. If another world exists."

"How do you know that?"

"I just know." Jess pushed a black button on a monitor housed in a grey enamelled case. A light flashed and numbers clicked on a counter. She twisted a dial and a green light came on. On the wall near the door she found a yellow handle on a semicircular plate with degrees marked on it. Another handle was marked with points of the compass. She tried the first and with well-geared ease the dome split and a slit of sky appeared. She tried the other; the dome and telescope rotated majestically.

"Should you touch that?"

"It's okay, don't worry." Jess closed the dome and reset the horizontal control. "Let's have another look in the office."

A bright fluorescent tube lit the office when Jess found the switch. She went to the desk. An old computer, not modern like the colourful ones in O'Malley, but grey and boxy with a small screen. A ledger book or journal with figures and writing on top of a filing cabinet. On the desk was a flat rectangular object about the size of a large book. Cables emerged from it and disappeared behind the desk to a collection of ancient electrical double adaptors of types Jess had never seen, not even since her move to O'Malley.

Wilfred was behind the partition looking at the photos again.

"Wilfred, do you know what this thing is?"

He came out with a piece of yellowed newspaper in his hand. "It looks like something from Ivan's world. Everything is probably like that there. Have a look at this," he said, but Jess wasn't interested. She was at the outside door.

"How long until it gets dark?" It was later than she'd thought. Sleep, and the late lunch had skewed her sense of time. The sky over the eastern hills was losing its colour and the buildings' shadows extended past the dirt road to the edge of the plateau and mingled with shadowy trees.

"Let's go back to the house until it gets properly dark. Ivan and Cassie should be back soon. You could ring your—mother—in Willowvale, maybe," said Wilfred.

"Mmmm," said Jess. For some reason she didn't want to call Mother just now. "I'll take something from here to read. There's nothing to do in the house." She picked up the journal from the filing cabinet, and a book with big shiny photographs from a bookshelf that was squeezed into a corner near the door. They closed the observatory door and walked across to the house. On such a cloudless evening there was no spectacular sunset, but a slow fading of the world from bright to subdued; from summer blue through faint yellows, oranges, reds and purples toward the velvety dark blue it would be when night fell.

Jess stood aside to let Wilfred enter the house first. That was interesting. There was no problem getting back into the house. She stopped on the doorstep to take a look at the scene. She knew that somewhere past those hills was the road between Willowvale and O'Malley—but she didn't know if she cared.

Inside, the lights flickered slowly. Jess made them change at her will a couple of times to see if she could. She held her breath for as long as possible to see what would happen. The UHF radio beeped and crackled. Wilfred had already filled the old kettle and was trying to light the stove with a flint. "There's not much variety but plenty of it," he said, looking in the pantry cupboard. Jess handed him some matches from the shelf and sat down at the table. Wilfred brought a teapot and cups and poured tea to which he added sweetened condensed milk from a tin. "I've been thinking about the professor. Do you think she's really blind?"

"Impossible to tell," said Jess, blowing on the scalding tea.

"I think she is blind, or nearly blind, and she's adapted amazingly well. But there are things around—"

"—that only a seeing person could use." Jess finished the sentence.

"There are three possibilities. One: she's not really blind, but pretending. Two: she's magic. Three: someone else is involved."

"These lights are getting to me. Let's drink our tea outside."

They watched carefully and safely exited the kitchen onto the small porch. It was unclear from this side of the house which world they were in. The sky grew darker. Birds made evening calls. They leaned against the steps. Faint stars appeared.

Some time later, inside, even Jess was feeling concerned about Cassie,

Ivan and the professor. The lights continued to flicker at a moderately calm rate, not bothering her too much; or at least, she was a bit more used to it. Jess looked at the photos in the book and thought that no alternate world—and she still wasn't fully convinced that one really existed—could be as exciting as this vast jewelled sky, the one that was not confined to the book, but all around for as far as one could imagine.

Wilfred picked up the various communications devices and idly pressed buttons. His perso-text had slowly recharged, and while they were in the observatory had printed out several disjointed messages. "It's probably good that I can't quite read Mum's messages." he said.

Jess was reading, and said, "Mmm."

"I guess I should send her a message so she doesn't worry," he said.

"Tell her we're at Mother's place. Marilyn Bagshaw's. That'll shut her and Daddy up." said Jess.

"Can you…make it stop flashing for a bit?"

Jess held her breath. The light stabilized. Wilfred hurriedly entered a message and turned the "send" handle just as Jess couldn't hold her breath any longer.

"There. I hope that's okay."

"You are a good boy," Jess said carelessly. She saw Wilfred blush and turn away. "Sorry. I meant you're so…nice. I mean, good, really good. She's your mother. I can't say I care what Daddy thinks. She'll tell him anyway. He'd be too gutless to go back to Willowvale, but at least…he won't worry."

"What do they see in each other?"

"At least your mother—I mean ours, Berenice—is tough enough to stand up to him. Not like my mother—I mean stepmother. Marilyn. I'm sorry, Wilfred, but I can't think of Berenice as my mother."

"I hope she's strong enough. Why can you do that?" said Wilfred, changing the subject abruptly, as the light flickered in its regular pattern.

"I don't know." Jess didn't want to think about it. She was trying to make sense of the journal, which had entries going back over twenty years.

"Do it again,"

"It's probably something to do with what happened when I went outside." Jess was starting to feel quite fond of Wilfred. The bond they had from suffering from the misbehaviour of their two unpleasant parents, perhaps. She liked him, and it was a long time since she'd felt that way about anyone. A brother was a nice relaxing thing to have. Obligingly she held her breath.

Wilfred's perso-text whirred and beeped. "She says…" Wilfred began to say when the phone rang. Jess let her breath out. The phone cut its ringing and the perso-text tape stuttered.

"Again," said Wilfred.

"Why?"

"Who on earth would ring here? Who would even know the number?"

"Someone must. Why else would she have all these phones and the radio and stuff?"

"Yeah. And the only logical explanation of the computer and books and paintings is…"

"Maybe she did all that before she lost her sight."

"No. This looks quite new. It's still wet." Wilfred peered closely at the painting on the easel.

"Don't answer if it rings again."

"Why not?"

"I don't know. I've got a bad feeling about it." Jess returned to the book of photos.

The phone rang again. Despite her bad feeling, Jess held her breath. Wilfred picked up the receiver.

"Don't talk," said Jess. The lights flickered.

"Jess! It cut off."

"Don't. You can listen. If they ring again."

The phone rang again. Almost, but not quite involuntarily, this time Jess held her breath, giving Wilfred a stern look. He picked up the phone. Jess heard a faint voice. A man.

"Hello? Professor? Are you all right? What's wrong?"

Wilfred remained silent.

The voice became rapidly more alarmed. Just as Jess couldn't hold her breath any longer, the man said, "I'll be there soon."

The call cut off as Jess said, "You fool. What have you done? Someone's coming now."

Wilfred slammed the phone down. "He was already worried about her. He'd probably come anyway. You wanted me to pick up the phone."

Their quarrel, if it was to become one, was interrupted by voices and footsteps outside and a heavy thud on the porch. Jess heard Cassie call urgently, "Ivan, come and help. Wilfred, Jess…where are they? I hope they're okay."

Ivan said, "Is she dead?" as Jess hurried across the room. She tried to open the door but something blocked it. "I can't open the door."

Wilfred was beside her. There was scuffling and dragging and Ivan said, "Try now."

The door opened easily now. The flashing light sped up so that Jess saw a jerky vision of Ivan, dirtier and more bedraggled than ever, and Cassie with her hair spread out from her head like an explosion. On the floor at their feet lay the limp figure of Professor Fenella Carter.

"We have to get her inside."

Jess held her breath and watched as Wilfred, Cassie and Ivan struggled to lift and drag the professor inside. The professor's face was like crumpled paper and her hands dangled bonily. Jess felt faint. The light flashed wildly.

"Is she dead?"

"Gently—"

"What happened?"

Jess closed the door and leaned against it, panting desperately, trying to get air, trying to control her heartbeat.

"She's not dead," said Ivan, "I think. I don't know."

Jess saw the others around the professor's still figure. Ivan held her wrist. "I thought I had her pulse."

"I'd forgotten this flashing light," said Cassie.

Jess felt faint, dizzy. The light flickered faster and faster.

CHAPTER EIGHTEEN
THE ASSISTANT

"We found the professor," said Cassie rather unnecessarily.

"Not again," Jess couldn't stop herself from saying, even though it was strangely difficult for her to speak. It took a huge effort to fill her lungs and get the words out. The kitchen light flashed wildly, and the effect made her feel more ill than she could have imagined. It was like two groups of bad musicians playing different tunes at the same time, with different rhythms and tones fighting each other ruthlessly into chaos, inside her head. This did not seem to affect the others at all. They fussed around the professor.

The light bulb failed with a crack.

"That's sort of good," said Ivan in the darkness that followed.

"Yeah, it was annoying," said Wilfred.

"Are there any candles?" said Cassie.

Jess didn't understand the conversation. What did they mean by it "was" annoying? It was still annoying to such an extent that she couldn't stand it. She had to get out. She groped her way along the wall to the hallway and to the front door.

It was difficult to tell whether the fluttering switching that had been made visible by the electric light was part of the wider world as it had been before. Jess watched from the doorway. The sky was an expanse of deep blue, punctuated by stars made faint by the full moon now hovering to the west. There was no way of telling if it was one sky, or two. She wanted to be back in Willowvale, where she knew how things worked.

Jess remembered the observatory. Even with that moon, perhaps it would be dark enough to see something through the telescope. *Can I get out with this…this…*she had no word for the rapid irregular change between the worlds that she could feel but not see.

Someone struck a match in the kitchen and the glow of a candle appeared. Jess flattened herself by the door. She didn't want the others to come looking for her. She concentrated on the timing of the vibrations between the two worlds—if that's what the feeling was. She tried to see the two motorbikes outside to gauge which world was which, but the rapid switches and the moonlit shadows were too confusing.

In the kitchen she thought she heard someone say, "Where's Jess?"

She held her breath and for a moment thought the fighting between the two worlds reduced.

The kitchen door opened. Quick as lightning Jess jumped out and fell in the dust of the driveway. She was afraid to look back at the door; she lay in the deep moonshadow of the house, trying to calm herself. The distressing vibrations had ceased. Slowly she sat up. Nobody came to the door, which had swung shut. It must have been her imagination, that somebody spoke of her. Evidently she had jumped into one world or the other, not into that horrible double-double world where she'd fainted this afternoon. But which world? She brushed the dust off her dress and stood up, feeling a little better. She wanted to look through the telescope at the endless sky. Her heart was still beating fast, but it was with excitement now. She crossed the driveway and went into the observatory.

It was different inside by herself. Jess switched on the office light and went through to the telescope room. The telescope seemed to wait for her like a gigantic but friendly creature. With hands trembling from unaccustomed nervousness Jess turned the handle that opened the dome. A stripe of sky appeared, dotted with pale stars, tiny as daisies on the top of a hill. She crept to the eyepiece of the telescope and looked. Now the lights that were stars, or planets, danced fuzzily before her eyes. She found a wheel that adjusted the focus and sank down onto a stool placed handily below the telescope, transfixed with wonder.

Jess wasn't sure how long she'd been there. She knew that while she was watching, stars had moved across the lens of the telescope, changing almost imperceptibly. It was odd that Wilfred or even one of the others hadn't come looking for her, but if she had any thoughts of them, she assumed that they were either busy with the professor or had fallen asleep.

The sound built up gradually in the periphery of her hearing; she didn't notice it until it stopped. Jess jerked her eye away from the telescope in fright and knocked her nose painfully on the eyepiece. All alert to sounds outside, she froze.

Was someone leaving without telling her? No, the sound had been coming closer, not fading, and the reason she'd noticed it was because it had stopped. Someone arriving?

"What the flaming possum?" A man's voice. Footsteps approached outside. "Professor? How's it going? Are you all right?"

Jess wished she'd locked the door, which creaked slightly as it opened.

"I was worried about you, and I've come all the way from O'Malley for nothing," said the man peevishly. "What was going on when I rang?"

Jess heard him in the office. There was a sound of the pulling out of a chair and of something being put down. She looked around the telescope room. There was no other way out. Not that she had any reason to be afraid, but who could this be? She guessed he was the person who Wilfred deduced must be responsible for the things that didn't fit; the paintings, the books, the journal. She felt scared anyway.

A shadow fell into the telescope room and a figure appeared in the doorway. "Professor? Are you in here?"

Jess didn't answer.

The man came into the room. He was in the process of taking off a leather jacket. Jess sat frozen on the observation stool like a frightened rabbit.

The man's eyes adjusted to the dim light. Jess had never seen anyone look so surprised in her life. His mouth opened and shut without a sound.

Jess decided that attack was the best form of defence. "Who are you?"

"Who are you?" asked the man. "What are you doing here?"

"I asked first."

"I'm Professor Carter's assistant, but that's none of your business. You shouldn't be in here. Who are you? Where's the professor?"

Jess stood up and moved behind the telescope. The man was tall and well built, and she had no reason to trust him. "She's sick. The others are looking after her." This was weird. She wanted to go home.

"This area is restricted," said the man. "Can't you read?" He pointed to a notice that said *Staff Only*. "Take me to the professor. Have you called for help?"

"You're here, aren't you?"

"I need to see her. I'm here because she didn't talk to me when I rang.

It was a strange conversation. Stranger than usual."

"She didn't talk because she wasn't here. Something's wrong with her. She wandered off. The others went to find her. You should be thanking us. They went miles into the bush to find her and help her back. Wilfred didn't talk on the telephone because he was so surprised…"

"Wilfred?"

"My brother. He can't help it if he's got a silly name."

"Your brother?" The man put his hand to his head. "Look. Take me to the professor. That's enough for now."

Jess didn't quite trust the man. "Wait outside." She didn't want to leave the telescope and the enticing skies it revealed.

"Don't order me around."

"I won't come out unless you go first."

The man looked up at the open dome. "Have you touched the telescope? What next?" He closed the dome. "I don't need you to show me the way, but I can't leave you here. It's prohibited."

"I haven't done any harm."

"I promise you are safe. I won't hurt you."

"You'd better not. Wilfred's very protective."

"I can just imagine," muttered the man.

Cassie, Ivan and Wilfred tried and tried to get through on any of the communications in the kitchen. None would connect.

"It's weird. Jess and I got a call before you came back." Wilfred's perso-text had run out of paper tape now. It had received a series of single letters too scattered to read. "Mum saying come home," he muttered speculatively. The two-way radio crackled with static and the three telephones made broken tones. Cassie was relieved that the light bulb was broken, not flashing now.

"Jess can sort of control it," Wilfred said.

"That's weird," said Cassie, not really listening.

"Something to do with when she fainted." Wilfred couldn't explain. "I don't know how. She's been a long time."

"She's probably asleep in the spare room," said Cassie.

Ivan sat on the floor near the divan. The professor lay, breathing shallowly, her pulse weak. He wasn't going to make the mistake of leaving her unsupervised again, no matter how incapacitated she seemed. Occasionally she muttered a few words: "the data…I can't do it…why?" as if she was having a conversation with someone Ivan couldn't see.

Cassie and Wilfred opened a tin of the baked beans that were so plentiful in the cupboard. "I'll never eat baked beans again," Cassie said.

"Bet you will."

They were eating when they heard the stuttering sounds of a motor outside. Everyone froze, expecting a knock.

"Who can it be?" They were too tired to go and see.

"Probably the mysterious person who isn't blind."

A few minutes later there was the sound of a knock at the front door. Ivan went to open it and Cassie heard the front door open, and Jess' voice. "It's easy enough to get into the house. Getting out is the problem."

"I need to see Professor Carter."

Jess stayed on the doorstep, listening as the man who said he was Professor Carter's assistant went into the house. She couldn't face going in there again, couldn't endure the flashing between the worlds. Voices floated to her from the kitchen; the alarmed tones of the stranger, a note of panic in Cassie's voice. Outside the night was blue and peaceful. She felt a pull between the lure of the telescope, and the thought of going home to Willowvale and staying with Mother, being looked after, having things the way they used to be.

She saw the glint of metal. Motorbikes flashed in and out of view in the shadowy moonlight. "I could take one and ride to Willowvale," Jess thought. Cassie had taken the ignition key from her bike and Jess was reluctant to take Wilfred's bike. Although she could drive a car—she had a cute little blue car like a jelly bean in O'Malley; Daddy gave it to her for her birthday—she'd only ridden a motorbike once before. The stranger had left his key in the ignition. She wheeled the bike a couple of hundred metres down the track, hitched the narrow skirt of her dress up so she could mount the bike, and wished she had some boots, not bare feet. The motor started with ear-splitting contrast to the quiet of the evening and Jess rode unsteadily away.

CHAPTER NINETEEN
MEETING JACK

Reenie felt as if she had fallen into a fast-flowing river and was rushing helplessly through rapids, over waterfalls, past unimagined scenery. It was exciting, uncomfortable, wonderful, frightening and out of control all at the same time. There was no sign of it ending. First, the now ordinary-seeming excitement of moving to O'Malley to start university that had been looming for so long as the biggest thing on her horizon. Then, Cal appeared out of nowhere, bringing with him emotions that created serious rapids in this rushing river. The expressions on Mum and Dad's faces when they saw Cal gave Reenie a curious flash of insight into their feelings…but she was too busy with her own and Cal's to pay much attention.

By Friday the drama increased, with Ivan choosing that moment to go bush, Anna suddenly coming down with an out-of-season cold that she immediately gave to Mum, Gran having a fall and bruising herself so badly that Pop wouldn't leave her alone in the house, and Dad on call with the rural fire brigade while dry lightning strikes were happening in the hills, threatening, but strangely anticlimactic.

This was the weekend Reenie was meant to move to O'Malley.

"It's lucky you've got your driving licence," Mum croaked when Reenie reminded her of this. "You'll have to take yourself up to O'Malley. Ask Gran if you can borrow her car."

So Reenie and Cal were off to O'Malley in Gran's little hatchback, which was piled with Reenie's stuff for her room: a small room with a bed and desk in a large building like a beehive full of students, half of them new like herself but all probably more confident and cleverer and already knowing people and not in the middle of being washed down a raging river full of boulders.

"Can I drive?" Cal said, as they came into Stirling. Reenie was happy to let him even though she had no idea what kind of driving licence existed in his world nor indeed whether he had one.

Arrival at the dorm was chaotic and full of deeply complicated paperwork, explaining why her parents weren't there like the parents of all the other students, meeting so many new people Reenie was sure she'd never sort them all out, being shown to a room so small she thought it was a mistake, unpacking her stuff from the car, filling this room with her things, and eventually realizing that the reason she felt so exhausted and disoriented wasn't simply everything that had happened any more than it was hunger.

They dug out the box of groceries she'd brought and went to the communal kitchen.

"I could eat a horse," said Cal.

"How about some two-minute noodles?"

"Whatever they are. Yes."

The kitchen area was surprisingly empty. All the other new students had probably gone out for celebratory lunches with their parents. They found Reenie's allocated food locker and fridge shelf. The kitchen was actually a vast industrial space divided into smaller areas, each a self-contained kitchen. There was a loud crash from the adjoining alcove and voice said, "Oh, shit."

Reenie and Cal peered over the partition. A boy their age stood among the ruins of what had once been spaghetti bolognaise, the broken-off handle of a saucepan in his hand.

"Are you okay?"

"That was going to be dinner for the whole week. I was trying to get ahead."

Reenie didn't know what to say.

The boy put the handle down and held his hand out across the partition. "Nice to meet you anyhow. I'm Jack Redhill. Are you new students too? I'm going to be studying…"

"Redhill?" said Cal. "That's an unusual name."

"Yeah. There are heaps of us where I come from, though."

"Where's that?" asked Cal in what Reenie thought rather an odd manner.

"Not far away. Walagu. My parents couldn't wait to see the back of me since I told them I don't want to be a farmer. I don't want to drive from Walagu every day, so I'm living here. I have to get a part-time job to pay the rent."

"Who's your father?"

"Peter Redhill… Why?"

Reenie was embarrassed. "Cal, why are you asking all these questions? I'm Reenie Williams and this is Cal—" she stopped. She didn't know Cal's surname.

Cal gave her a look. "Phil Rainhart."

Jack didn't notice the distinction between Cal and Phil, or did not comment; Reenie had forgotten that Cal was funny about names. "Rainhart? That's another unusual name. There used to be a family called Rainhart round Walagu, but I think they've moved away. Are you from Walagu?" Reenie knew that Walagu was such a small place that it counted itself lucky to have a pub, a petrol station and a one-teacher school. Jack continued talking, partly to himself and partly because, evidently, he was the kind of person who talked all the time. "I should know you—how old are you? Where did you go to school? You would have been there at the same time…where did you say you were from?"

"I didn't."

"He's from Willowvale," said Reenie.

"Did you go to Willowvale High School? Or WCC? I went to St Francis' in O'Malley, that would explain why…" Jack was saying, when Cal interrupted.

"Do you have any aunts?"

"Aunts?" Jack's expression went from general social curiosity to a plainly written "is this guy all there?"

"Yeah." Cal suddenly seemed to realize he was acting oddly. "I…um… think I have some relations round Walagu but my family have sort of lost touch with them…" his sentence faded.

"I don't have any aunts," said Jack, "except for one. She died young."

Cal went pale and grasped Reenie's hand.

"Let's sit down," she said.

There was a table and chairs at the end of the alcove. Cal's hand trembled in hers. "What was your aunt's name?"

"I forget." said Jack rather evasively.

"When did she die?"

"Oh, it was years ago. Before I was born. My older brother was a baby. I know it must have been awful. They don't know that she actually died. Nobody really knows, but what else could have happened? I think she got lost in the bush. They've never found her body. It's wild out there west of Walagu. It was ages ago."

"Are you sure you don't remember her name?" Reenie asked. Cal had become very silent. She guessed it must be something to do with his family, but she was mystified.

"It was something unusual. Theresa—no. Thelma? Thadie? Theodora. That's it. My grandparents still haven't got over her disappearance, Dad says; they never talk about her. He doesn't much either."

Cal jumped up and left the room.

"Is he okay? I mean…" Jack stared after him.

Reenie stood up. When Jack started to say the names, the sounds connected in her mind. Th- Th- Th- like a stuttering lisp. Twenty-odd years… "I'd better see if he's all right. Where did you say your grandparents live?"

"Um, I didn't, but they live at Underhill Bend down on the river near Walagu. Why is he so interested in my family?" Jack was puzzled. "Why is he so…upset about my aunt? He could never have known her."

"I'm not sure." Reenie swayed. She was so hungry she felt almost ill, and on second thought, Cal was best left to work through whatever was bugging him, by himself; she hadn't the ability to help. "Let's get this cleaned up."

"Thanks."

Reenie grabbed an apple from her grocery box and ate it while Jack found a dustpan and mop. Before they'd finished cleaning up, Cal reappeared and silently started cooking enough two-minute noodles for all of them after studiously reading the instructions. He served the noodles and they sat at the table again.

"I'd really like to meet your grandparents. I'm very interested in the mystery of your aunt," he said carefully.

Jack's rather innocent face became wary. "I don't think they'd want to talk about it. You're not studying journalism or something are you?"

"Do you know if any of the Rainharts at all are still round Walagu, then?" Cal asked.

"I said. None any more. Just a family that left."

Cal ate a slippery strand of noodle, wiped his mouth with the back of his hand and said, "It's odd. I was asking about your aunt because there's a story like that in my father's family too. A…relation. There's some kind of mystery about him. That's why I was so interested. I think it happened about twenty years ago."

Reenie could see from the way Cal was talking that he was feeling his way with Jack, trying not to push too hard. His father's family? What was going on?

Jack said slowly, "Yes, now that you mention it. There was a guy who disappeared about the same time. Could have been one of the Rainharts. Maybe that's why the family moved away. I think it was a tragedy mixed up with what happened to my aunt. Some kind of scandal, or suspicion... I'm just guessing..."

Cal stiffened like a cat that has reached striking distance of a bird, then turned his attention to his lunch.

"What are you going to study?" Jack asked Reenie.

Most of her things were out of the car, and her room was habitable if not tidy to a standard that Mum or Gran would approve of. Reenie and Cal sat on the bed to survey their work.

"What are you going to do?"

"Thought I might move up here and get a job."

"I mean about what Jack said. I know it's been bothering you all afternoon. I've got some idea, but you'd better tell me exactly what you're stewing about."

"Thistle and Raven have never said anything about their families, except that they all died in the Disaster. That means they came from Walagu or Stirling, but they've never said even that, exactly."

"Nothing at all?"

"You've met them. Thistle's even less of a talker than Raven. But what if they came from this world? What if Jack and his family are my family?"

"You think this missing aunt of Jack's is Thistle? It's not the same name."

"Theodora. Thistle. More similar than a lot of names. Maybe she didn't like her name. Maybe it's a nickname. It can't be a coincidence that a Rainhart disappeared about the same time."

"She never said anything?"

"I didn't even know she had a brother."

If she does, thought Reenie. "So you think Jack's your cousin?" There was no resemblance between Cal and Jack that Reenie could see.

"I'd like to find out for sure."

"And you think this old Mr and Mrs Redhill are your grandparents? And all this time your mother thought they were dead in the Disaster? And your father might still have relatives too?"

"If it's true, they would all think Thistle and Raven have been dead for years."

"Are you going to ask Jack to introduce you to them?"

"No."

"Don't you want to meet them?"

"I want to meet them," said Cal slowly, his eyes on the sky through the high windows of the kitchen. "We can find them ourselves. I don't think Jack would be any use. He doesn't know much and he wants to protect them. He thinks I'm some nosy wannabe journalist trawling up the past and that they'll die of shock if I appear asking questions."

Uni didn't actually start till Tuesday next week, and they had to get Gran's car back soon because she'd be sure to to want it even if Pop and Mum didn't think she was well enough. Without consciously doing it, Reenie started to make a plan in her head to take Cal to this Underhill Bend farm that he was so interested in, and see if they could sort out the mystery that was bothering him. "Let's finish unpacking," she said. Cal helped in an absent kind of way, carrying the last bags and boxes, not appearing to hear when spoken to, with a dazed, other-worldly expression and his auburn hair standing wildly about his head in flames like the first time Reenie had seen him. She took him by the hand, out to the corridor, locked the door and they went to the car.

It wasn't a long drive to Walagu, and not much further to Underhill Road, a turnoff onto dirt that Reenie had never explored in a life spent living in Willowvale.

"What will Cassie think when she finds out about this?"

"How can she find out? I'll never see her again."

Reenie hadn't considered this. "What do you mean?"

"The chances of getting there or here are too small to bother even thinking about. I don't want to."

Reenie turned off at a line of letterboxes and a sign. Underhill Road was narrow and potholed. A pipit flew startled from the verge and off across a paddock. The road curved down the gentle eastern side of the river valley. Wild wooded hills loomed high on the western side. They passed over a grid. The road narrowed and turned abruptly at the corner of a paddock.

She stopped the car. Ahead was another sharp bend and a gate with a faded hand-painted sign:

Underhill Bend Farm Road. Private.

CHAPTER TWENTY
DEVELOPMENTS

Wilfred thought he was hallucinating when he saw Sinclair come into the room. The dim candlelight made him slow to be certain. He stood up, knocking over his chair. "Sinclair? What are you doing here?"

"The girl in the observatory told me you were here. Some cockatoo-and-bullfrog story about being your sister. Where's the professor?"

Ivan stood up too.

"You?" said Sinclair, considerably more surprised than he was when when he saw Wilfred.

"Me too," said Cassie.

"I must be going crazy," said Sinclair, aside. "What's wrong with the lights? Is there a blackout? I have to see the professor."

"She's not good," said Ivan warningly, as Sinclair hurried to the divan where the professor lay.

"Professor Fenella…"

The professor sat up. "Sinclair, how nice of you to come."

Wilfred, Cassie and Ivan stared. She had been unconscious.

"Can one of you make me a cup of tea? I'm parched. Two sugars, black. One for Sinclair too."

"She was unconscious."

"What's going on?" Sinclair asked the professor.

"I've got some new data on the terraspectromultiscope. It's important. I need you to analyze it."

Wilfred saw that Ivan and Cassie were too busy listening to this conversation to make the tea, so he put the kettle on the gas stove, which was not affected as the lights were. Sinclair and the professor continued in conversation, and no reasonable explanation of the situation presented itself to him. Sinclair was one of the Gentlemen of the Road, the bikie group that Wilfred had drifted away from last year. One of the saner Gentlemen, Wilfred thought, but still capricious and unreliable—not to be entirely trusted. Wilfred also knew that Sinclair was the manager of the hotel at the edge of the crater lake. A man of unexpected talents. Wilfred put tea leaves into the pot and sugar into two mugs. Sinclair could drink what he was given, he wasn't going to ask what he wanted.

As he poured hot water into the teapot, it dawned on Wilfred that again nothing had been heard of Jess for some time—not since he heard her talking to Sinclair at the door—and also that the world was no longer flashing and flickering.

He put the two teas down near Sinclair and the professor and shook Ivan's shoulder. "Where's Jess?" he whispered. Ivan shrugged.

"I'm feeling fine," Professor Carter said to Sinclair. "You worry too much."

"What's all this data you've got? Where is it from?"

Wilfred dragged Cassie and Ivan to the front door. "Jess isn't here. I heard her come in with Sinclair. Where is she?"

"She's probably out at the telescope. She said she wanted to look at the stars."

Somewhere outside there was the distant sound of an engine sparking to life. "What was that?" said Cassie loudly.

There was a jolt and a moment of complete silence.

"Swooping magpies, what was that?" said Sinclair from the kitchen.

"That was a motorbike." Wilfred flung the door wide open. "Jess has gone." He ran outside, hearing Cassie and Ivan call his name, but ignoring them and any danger he was entering.

They stumbled against him as they landed on the driveway, but Wilfred didn't pay any attention other than to shift his feet to regain his balance.

"Where are the bikes? She can't have taken all of them."

Ivan spoke slowly. "We're in my world. The bikes are in your world. They're not here."

"I heard her. She started an engine. She must have gone off—"

"If she took a bike, she must be in the other world, like Ivan said."

Sinclair came to the door. "What's going on?" He peered into the darkness. "Where's my bike? Where are all the bikes? What have you kids done with them? Am I *really* going mad?"

The professor, in her amazingly revived condition, stood behind Sinclair. "It's happened at last. Still, I'd like you to analyse the data I collected, Sinclair. Come on. The boy left the terraspectromultiscope in the house. You can take it to the computer in the office. It's quite heavy. I've carried it enough."

She took Sinclair's arm and drew him into the house, still protesting about his motorcycle. "That tall girl from O'Malley—the one I caught in the observatory—who is she? Did you know she was a delinquent? And what's happened to the other bikes? Who else knows about this place?"

The professor's voice was soothing. "Don't you worry. It will be fine."

Sinclair's and the professor's voices faded into the house. Wilfred and the others stood huddled on together on the drive. The front door closed with a bang and in the darkness Wilfred gradually became aware of a spectacular array of stars overhead, the Milky Way sweeping over them like an enormous arch.

Something beeped like a cricket, and Ivan reached into his pocket and brought out a small rectangular object that Wilfred knew was his version of a perso-text. Ivan called it a phone, but it bore no resemblance to a real telephone: no earpiece, no curly cord, no round dial with holes in it for your finger. It must have been some kind of…who cared? Ivan did something to his device's glass screen, which had lit up brightly, and Wilfred saw neat writing appear.

"It's from Reenie."

"Is she with Pip? Where are they?"

"She says—this is weird—she says…"

"Just read it to us," said Cassie impatiently, trying to see over Ivan's shoulder.

"It says, *Hey Ivan, you'll never guess—*"

"Is this important?" said Wilfred, who was very worried about Jess, and curious to find out what Sinclair and the professor were up to.

"*—you'll never guess who Cal and I are with -*"

"Of course we won't," said Cassie.

"*Cassie would be VERY EXCITED,*" read Ivan with emphasis.

"Go on."

Even Wilfred was interested now.

"I'm trying to read it, but people keep interrupting. *Very Excited, if only there was a way of telling her. We've found some people called Vi and Herb Redhill and they—*"

"What? What? Who are they?" interrupted Cassie breathlessly.

"*They are Thistle's parents!*" Ivan read.

Cassie was not the kind of person who shrieked. She took in a sharp breath and grabbed Wilfred's arm so tightly it hurt. "Where are they? How did she find them? Can we see them?" she whispered. "Is it true? How can it be? Let's go there."

"She doesn't say where they are."

Ivan busily entered a message into his device. *Cassie knows. She's here with me, Wilfred and Jess. There's another way through.* Wilfred felt sorry for Cassie. Suddenly he remembered the ancient newspaper article he'd found in the observatory. He rummaged through his pockets. Cassie continued to ask question after question. Ivan entered letters into his text-phone on what looked like miniature typewriter keys that appeared on his glass screen. Inside the house, Wilfred heard the voices of Sinclair and the professor; his mind churned with questions about them, and Jess, and even himself. He felt the crumpled newspaper in his back pocket.

"Cassie. Read this."

"It's dark, you pickled bluetongue."

"Are you turning into Jess?" asked Wilfred hastily, and instantly regretted it. He felt Cassie flinch, and remembering Jess somewhere out there, felt disloyal. Jess was out in the other world, struggling with whatever impulsive disaster she'd got herself into (with what, from the engine sound, he guessed was Sinclair's large and very powerful motorcycle rather than his or Cassie's smaller ones) and that annoying as Jess was, he already loved his sister of twenty-four hours. "Sorry, Cassie," he said.

Cassie snatched the newspaper from him. "We'll have to go inside if I'm to read this."

They went to the back door, as the front was locked now. Faint yellow candlelight showed through the glass pane. "Let's stay out here," said Wilfred. Sitting on the step, Cassie held the frayed yellowing paper in the light of Ivan's phone-text device and read out loud:

> **"Mystery of Missing Teenagers. An extensive search for teenagers Rowan Rainhart and Theodora Redhill has been**

conducted over the past three weeks under the coordination of police and emergency services. Family, friends, fire rescue and members of the public have assisted with the search in the Walagu area. The teenagers went missing separately on Saturday 20th January and have not been seen since. Serious concerns are held for their safety. The young people originate from the vicinity of Walagu and Underhill Bend. Hopes continue that they will be found safe and well, but the lack of clues as to their whereabouts is causing very serious concern as to their safety. Rowan and Theodora were last seen in the vicinity of the Walagu Ranges…

"That must be Thistle and Raven! It matches Reenie's story!"

"What newspaper is it?" asked Ivan.

"The *O'Malley Times*," said Wilfred, looking over Cassie's shoulder.

"No such paper," said Cassie. "I've only heard of the *O'Malley Weekly* and the *O'Malley News*."

"I think the *O'Malley Times* went out of business before I was born," said Wilfred.

"The O'Malley Times is still going strong. It's the only newspaper in O'Malley. I've never heard of the *Weekly* or the *News*," said Ivan.

"Don't you see! Thistle and Raven went missing from this world, Ivan's one; or at least, they went missing before the Disaster, when there was only one world! The point where the world split! Maybe they still have relations here in this world that we don't know about. Maybe they've always hoped that Thistle and Raven will come back one day, and now Pip and Reenie have found them!" She consulted the cutting again. "Underhill Bend. I don't know it."

That was logical, Wilfred thought, knowing that Cassie had never left Willowvale before last year, and then only once under dark and difficult conditions. Even if she had travelled more, there was no way she could have known the area; any farm on the river near Walagu would be long destroyed and deep under the crater lake that replaced Walagu and its surroundings.

Ivan said, "There's an Underhill Road between Stirling and Walagu. It goes down toward the river. you can see a farm from the highway, up across the river. I've never been there, though."

"We can go there now, and meet them, and then we can get Thistle and Raven up here and take them there…"

"Don't count your chickens before they're hatched," said Ivan in an automatic kind of way.

Wilfred, who had been listening with half an ear to sounds in the kitchen, held up his hand. "Shh."

"Calm down, Wilfred, they don't care what we do," said Cassie.

"I can hear something else."

"It's just the professor and Sinclair talking. Why is he here?" said Ivan.

"Can you be quiet for a second?" Wilfred was sure he heard footsteps crunching nearby.

A moment later Jess came round the corner and onto the porch. "Before you ask, I changed my mind," she said, sighed, and sat down on the step with Cassie. "I don't know what I want."

"How did you get here?" asked Wilfred.

"That guy's bike is too big. I couldn't control it. I nearly came off the thing. I'd only gone maybe a kilometre. Not even that far. I stopped. Turned it off. Everything was quiet; so quiet. I thought about your story about the two worlds, and wondered what the other one is like. If it exists. Then I felt—thunder or an earth tremor or a tree falling nearby or something—I thought I was getting ill again, like this afternoon. I was scared. I was too scared to start the bike up again. It's too big, too heavy to ride. I'm exhausted."

Wilfred put his arm around Jess' shoulders and felt her breathing heavily and fast.

"It wasn't what I expected. I thought I knew what I wanted," said Jess cryptically. Wilfred didn't know what she meant.

"Jess," said Ivan, "How did you get back here?"

"I walked up the road. Like I said."

"But this is the other world," said Cassie. "You can't have."

"I'm here, aren't I? I'm not fully convinced that there's any such thing as another world." Jess examined her feet, which were bare and scratched. Her party dress was crushed and torn with a dark streak of grease across the skirt.

There was a silence on the porch during which Wilfred heard the professor and Sinclair's voices from inside, and the faint call of a night bird far across the plateau.

"It's great that you're back, Jess, and all that," said Cassie. "Now let's go and find my grandparents, and Pip."

"You and your Pip. Don't you ever think of anyone but yourself?" said Jess.

"You can't talk. You stole the bike to go home to your mansion. Spoilt brat with your satin shoes and party dress and your rich daddy. Running home to mummy."

"Shut up. You know nothing."

"Pip's my brother. I care about him. You're too selfish to care about anyone but yourself."

"Pip's sick of you. He probably left Willowvale to get away from you."

"How dare you?"

"I bet he felt smothered by your sugary hero-worship. You should leave him alone. Let him get on with things. You need to get a life. You're always bossing other people around because you are totally boring yourself."

Cassie stood, speechless with rage. Wilfred thought she was going to hit Jess. "Cassie, we can't just take Sinclair's bike," said Wilfred, desperate to break the tension, "Not again," he added, realizing Jess was bristling just as spikily. "Anyway, it can only carry two people."

Cassie opened her mouth to argue when the door opened, bumping Ivan.

"I thought I heard voices," said Sinclair. He saw Jess. "Where's my motorcycle?"

"It's out the front," said Jess shortly.

"You lot better come in before you get up to some other mischief."

Cassie drew in a breath as though she would object but Wilfred didn't hear any more from her as he followed Jess and Sinclair inside. The kitchen was lit by the candle, now burnt low and dripping with wax; shadows darker than any outside filled every corner. Through the uncurtained window he once more saw the sky flicker almost imperceptibly every second or so. He felt trapped. He was weary of this dingy kitchen and the half-ruined house with its dust and broken windows.

The professor sat at the table like a queen or a judge with the old journal Jess had found in the observatory in front of her.

"Why did you run away, girl?"

Jess, still angry, snapped, "Because I wanted to."

The lenses of Professor Carter's black glasses flashed candlelight as she moved her head. Sinclair was a looming shadow figure standing behind the professor, his face creepily uplit. Wilfred felt like shrinking back into the shadows where Ivan and Cassie were silently lurking, but he was reluctant to move and attract attention.

The professor turned her face away from Jess and to the window so precisely that Wilfred could have sworn she saw. She said, "I can't feel it any more. Can you?"

"Of course I can feel it," said Jess irritatedly.

What? Thought Wilfred, then realized they spoke of the switch in the sky which had been so bothersomely connected to Jess earlier. She showed no sign of being distressed by it now.

Once more the professor turned and faced Jess, perhaps in surprise. Her face was impassive. She held her hands out toward Jess. Again Wilfred was reminded of someone of immense dignity and importance—a monarch or priestess—but dangerous. "Come closer, girl. I've been waiting for you."

Jess, puzzled, curious, reluctant, flattered, scared…Wilfred could not accurately read her unspoken emotions, slowly approached the professor as if drawn by a thread. The professor continued to hold her hands out toward Jess, and Jess, as if impelled by an invisible force, walked forward and put both her hands onto the professor's. The older woman started as Jess touched her. "I can feel…yes, it's you. I've waited for so long." Her voice was so quiet that Wilfred thought he imagined hearing the words. Softer than his own breathing or Sinclair's. Jess was silent. The candle flickered with some small movement of air and Wilfred felt a line of sweat run down his back.

"You came back. You feel the worlds." The professor smiled, her face pleating into elaborate radiating wrinkles emphasised by the candlelight. "I can give it all to you now."

"But I can only feel it by accident," said Jess.

"The end is more important than the means. Don't worry. It will be wonderful."

"I need to think." Jess' voice was as quiet as the professor's and unusually uncertain. "I want…wanted…to go home to Willowvale. To my mother…stepmother. To have things the same as they used to be."

"Really? The girl who spent the evening staring at stars, after breaking into the observatory, and stealing my private journal to see what this place was all about?"

"I didn't steal it. I wanted to know."

"So, do you want to be an astronomer? Learn my trade? Or do you want to go back to Willowvale and be ordinary? Boring?"

The strain of listening to this made Wilfred's ears hurt. Somewhere not far away a noise broke his concentration. An engine.

"No, not again!" yelled Sinclair, running toward the front door.

Wilfred spun around. Cassie and Ivan weren't in the shadows behind him. They were gone.

CHAPTER TWENTY-ONE
SWITCHES

Ivan clung to Cassie's back, his eyes squeezed shut, the lyrics of a corny country song that Dad often sang churning through his head. *I started home 'tween twelve and one, I cried "Oh God, what have I done?"* What had they done indeed? *Stolen Sinclair's bike in another world...to solve a mystery decades old;* his mind concluded without his permission. How had he got himself into this situation? Why had he gone along with this hare-brained madness? Leaving Wilfred and Jess behind—he groaned out loud at the thought— with the professor and Sinclair, neither of whom he entirely trusted. He still hadn't worked out exactly what was going on with Wilfred and Jess. It was almost impossible to believe that they were brother and sister. All of these thoughts, however, were distractions from the physical situation. Sinclair's motorcycle must have been nearly the weight of a small car, and designed to travel fast. Ivan and Cassie together weighed possibly about the same as Sinclair by himself. The track down from the observatory was okay for walking or Cassie's small trail bike, or an off-road vehicle like Dad's ute, travelling slowly. Not so good for a heavy road bike driven by a novice. With a passenger.

The bike lurched alarmingly and Ivan opened his eyes to see a dizzying pass of trees in the headlight. God. They didn't even have helmets. Cassie managed to retain control. Ivan forced himself to open his eyes, which had shut involuntarily. It was difficult to work out where they were, but he thought he recognized the place where he'd bumped into Cassie last night, the campsite by the creek in the lush little valley. Even though they'd been in the other version of the world then, it looked the same in both. From there it was not far to the road that at normal times seemed rough and narrow but now would be neat and civilized by comparison to this goat-track. Resigning himself to his state of complete powerlessness and to his churning thoughts, Ivan closed his eyes again and prayed to survive.

"Mum. It's Reenie."

"My throat's terrible. I can't talk. When will you be home?" Mum still sounded dreadful.

"I won't be home tonight. It's a long story but …"

"I'm stuck here with a sore throat, Anna in front of the TV watching a full series of *Hunter Street,* sniffing every three seconds; Pop's had to take Gran to the doctor…and Mick's been at Fire Control since seven this morning. Start talking. I need the entertainment."

Mum can talk well enough if she wants, Reenie thought. "To cut a long story short…" she began.

"I've got all the time in the world," Mum interrupted.

Reenie wished she'd called on her mobile, and could say she was running out of credit, or that her battery was going flat or reception was terrible. But she couldn't. She was calling from Mr and Mrs Redhill's home phone. "I heard from Ivan," she said to distract Mum for a moment.

"Is that ratbag still alive? Tell him not to come home until he's civilized. So. This long story?" Mum may well have been sick, but her brain was working fine.

"It's like this. We met this guy and he's turned out to be Cal—I mean Phil's—long-lost cousin, and we've found Cal —Phil's grandparents who he thought…"

"Long-lost cousin? Grandparents?" Mum's croak was sceptical.

Reenie faltered. The further into the story she got, the less credible it sounded, even to her. "And his grandparents thought his mother was dead for the last twenty years. They didn't know he even exists, and they've asked us to stay the night, and it's getting late."

"I know perfectly well that it's getting late, Irini."

Oh no. Her full name. A cliché, but Mum never used her full name unless she was becoming dangerous. "And his grandparents want us to stay the night…"

"Reenie. Exactly where are you, really? I want the truth."

Mum thought she was making the whole thing up, but this was the truth. "I'm at Phil's grandparents' farm. Un-der-hill Bend," she said with sarcastically clear diction.

"Reenie. There's no need for that. Do these—" Reenie almost heard Mum say the word "mythical" "—grandparents and cousins have names?"

"Of course they do, Mum." It was ironic that the moment she was telling the exact truth was the moment Mum chose to doubt everything she said. "Mr and Mrs Redhill. Vi and Herb. Jack's the cousin."

There was a pause while Mum coughed. "Redhill? Do I know them?" That was a rhetorical question. Mum was one of those people who knew pretty much everybody.

Mrs Redhill came into the hall with a mug of cocoa. "Here you are, dear. I know it's a hot night, but I always say a warm cocoa helps you sleep," she said shakily.

"Thanks, Mrs Redhill."

Mum's end of the phone exuded astonished silence.

"Well, I'll say good night," said Reenie. "Bye, Mum." She held off hanging up the phone until after Mrs Redhill said, "You can have Theodora's room. I'll put Cal into Peter's old room. Sleep well."

Wilfred's perso-text indicated an incoming message. He pressed the "delay" button and wondered what to do. The professor's communications corner had every kind of device. Maybe there was some perso-tape there. Jess and the professor were deep in conversation. Sinclair had run outside after Cassie, Ivan and his motorbike. Wilfred didn't care what Sinclair did. He wouldn't catch up with Ivan and Cassie unless they crashed the bike immediately. Wilfred hoped they wouldn't do that, even though he couldn't believe that they'd run off like that. Jess was fully involved with the professor. Cassie had her long-lost family and her quest for her brother, and Ivan had Cassie. He felt even more alone than before.

His fingers found a roll of perso-tape in the dark, and he put it into the perso-text. The whirr of its printout was quiet. He felt a long snake of paper emerge. It was too dark to read the code so he put the tape into his pocket and went outside. This weekend was the weirdest and most unbalanced of his whole life, including the one last year when he'd first met Cassie and Ivan.

"All I wanted was to see Cassie again," he thought. He didn't want to read his perso-texts, which would surely be Mum asking where he and Jess were, and perhaps Dale or Alistair asking him if he wanted to meet up at the Pink Elephant or the Crazy Parrot for an alco-tail-sundae. Next time they asked, he'd go with them. He'd talk to the next girl they bet he wouldn't dare to speak to, as well, no matter how pretty or plain she was.

Not caring which world he ended up in, nor about anything else much, Wilfred quietly opened the back door and melted out into the velvety summer night.

"Which way?" Cassie stopped at the old landmark tree that marked the intersection of the fire trail and the back road to Willowvale. She and Ivan both put a foot down and managed to stop the bike from toppling.

There was no point arguing with Cassie nor trying to suggest a more sensible approach. Ivan, hoping the next leg of the trip would be less terrifying, pointed in the direction that would take them to Underhill Road.

The going was better from here. Still unsealed, but a proper road, not just grass and bushes growing between wheel ruts. They came near the intersection with West Underhill Road. Ivan tapped Cassie's shoulder, their agreed signal to turn off. In the distance he saw the halo of light polution from Willowvale's street lights glowing in the sky. How odd that down there, life was going on as normal.

Reenie lay awake in the bed that had been Cal's mother's when she was Cassie's age. She supposed Cal was on the other side of the bedroom wall, hearing as she did the muffled sounds of Mr and Mrs Redhill talking to each other as they went to bed. A mosquito whined around her head. The old woollen blanket was heavy and hot. She wanted to turn on the light and look at the room again; the room that was unchanged since the day the teenage Thistle left it. She wanted to knock on the wall and hear Cal's answer, but she didn't want to disturb his grandparents, who had become quiet now.

She thought back to their arrival. Underhill Farm Road after the last turnoff was narrow and potholed between dusty yellow grass that grew as high as the car windows. The road curved down the gentle eastern side of the river valley. Wild, wooded hills loomed high on the western side. They passed over a grid. The road narrowed and turned abruptly at the corner of a paddock.

Reenie stopped the car. Ahead was another sharp bend and a gate with a faded hand-painted sign: *Private Property*. Cal got out and opened the gate, carefully closing it after the car passed. The road narrowed to two rutted tyre marks separated by a strip of grass that brushed the belly of the car. They crossed the river by a low wooden bridge that rattled alarmingly under the tyres. The farm yard, blocked by another gate, was filled with piles of firewood and rusting farm machinery. Dogs barked. The farmhouse was hidden behind a row of overgrown cypress pines, only its iron roof visible. Behind it was a windbreak of eucalypts and European trees. Hens scratched around the rusty scrap piles. Despite the hotness of the afternoon, a faint line of smoke extended from a chimney into the still air.

They got out of the car. A man's voice could be heard from behind the cypresses, ordering the dogs quiet. Reenie heard the sound of chains, and a border collie burst onto the driveway, followed by an old kelpie, grey around the muzzle. When the dogs saw Cal and Reenie they recommenced barking. The man approached with an arthritic step. A door slammed and a woman called out, "Herb? Who is it?"

Herb was a compact man in his seventies with a fringe of white hair beneath a battered felt hat, dressed in work trousers and a checked shirt. He said, "Visitors," without looking at them. When he came within a couple of metres of the gate, he growled at the dogs, who put their tails between their legs and slunk behind him. He looked up, saying, "Didn't you see the sign? This is private property. I s'pose you'll say you're lost? This road doesn't go anywhere."

"We're not lost. We've come to see you," said Cal quietly. "I'm Cal Rainhart-Redhill."

"Herb, Herb, when will you learn to be polite?" said the woman, following Herb down the drive.

Herb was silent, his face pale, his mouth open. Cal was in the same condition. The woman looked as much like Thistle (but twenty-odd years older) as Cassie looked like a younger version of her.

"Mr and Mrs…Redhill?" said Reenie.

The man bent and took hold of the dogs' collars. The woman came closer. "Herb, what's wrong? Are you all right?" Confused, she looked from him to the visitors. She saw Cal. Her mouth fell open the way Herb's had, but she gathered her self-possession faster. "Who are you?" She ran past the man and the dogs.

"Cal Rainhart-Redhill," he repeated.

Herb and the woman pressed themselves up to the gate. Both the old people looked as if they might faint. The dogs whined uneasily.

"Rainhart? Redhill?"

"My mother is Thistle Redhill."

"You're Theodora's child? Where is she? Is she coming? Is she alive?" said Herb. His fingers whitened as his grip on the gate intensified. "Vi? What's happening?"

"Can we come in?" asked Reenie.

The woman fumbled with the gate catch. The man held the dogs by their collars. Vi took Cal by both hands and searched his face with greedy eyes.

It was hot and stuffy in the house. Reenie felt trapped by the crowding furniture. Cal's hand grasped hers. Vi muttered something about a cup of tea and left the room. Herb stood silently on the hearthstone of the empty fireplace—*the smoke must be from a kitchen chimney*, Reenie found herself thinking irrelevantly—looking shocked, disbelieving and hopeful all at the same time.

Herb, after kicking the dust off his boots onto the hearth, and pushing his hat back to scratch his head, causing the hat to fall backwards onto the mantelpiece, then further, taking a copper ashtray and a swan made of starched crochet-work with it, shuffled his feet and directed a long, unblinking stare at Cal. Herb looked down, coughed, and said, "I reckon it's true. You don't look as much like our Theodora as you might, but I can see her in you. Where's she been all these years? Why hasn't she contacted us? Why isn't she here, too? Who's your father? That young bloke that disappeared, I suppose. The name rings a bell."

"Raven," said Cal, "I mean Rowan Redhill."

"Silly a name as Thistle," said Herb. "Thistle. I haven't heard that name a long time. She always called herself Thistle. Silly to name yourself after a prickly weed…we never moved from this place, always hoped she'd come back, even when they told us she was dead and gone forever. You can't stop yourself from hoping…" He fell silent again, not appearing to expect a reply, turning to pick up his hat and the items that had fallen, and rearrange them on the mantel.

It was understandable, given country hospitality and everything else that Vi and Herb wanted them to stay, but Reenie wished she was at home, or even in her room in O'Malley. She was tired, but her mind raced. She slapped ineffectually at the mosquito and lay gazing into the blackness that hid the ceiling.

Reenie didn't know how long she'd been dozing when something woke her. She sat up, forgetting for a moment where she was, the unfamiliar room blending with a confused dream. She registered the sound of a vehicle approaching. The dogs moved around in their kennels. It was difficult to hear more distant sounds. At the moment Reenie was sure she heard something coming, the dogs began to bark. She jumped up and dragged on her clothes. From the window she saw a light shining through the trees between the front gate and the house. In gaps where the dogs paused for breath she heard the motor stop, and voices.

Mr and Mrs Redhill stirred in their room.

Cal came in, dishevelled. "What's going on?"

"How would I know?"

He joined her at the window. Mr Redhill shouted at the dogs and Reenie heard Mrs Redhill say, "Are you sure you need to get the gun out?"

The gun? thought Reenie. The dogs stopped barking and she heard the voices again. They sounded familiar. She grabbed Cal's arm. "We've got to stop him from shooting at them. It sounds like Ivan's voice—"

Cal, also listening intently, said at the same time, "Cassie's out there too. How did she get here?"

They ran to the front door. Mr Redhill was fumbling with the key to a gun cabinet in the living room. Mrs Redhill peered through the curtains. In the second during which Reenie wondered desperately what to do, Cal dashed past and out the door. Reenie followed him into the cool night. "Herb!" she heard Mrs Redhill shout. She ran after Cal to the yard gate, hoping not to be accidentally shot, hearing the dogs bark frantically over the old people's voices.

Now that Wilfred was out of the observatory house, he had a feeling of freedom. He felt his way down the road that he'd come up with Jess last night. He was amazed that he'd managed to get his motorbike into this other world, and that he'd left Jess at the observatory with the professor and Sinclair.

Past the fire trail, the road was much better in this world than at home. Wilfred saw signs of Cassie and Ivan's passing in marks on the dusty road. He guessed he was quite close to the main road between Willowvale and O'Malley when he began to doubt the wisdom of this ride. Even in this world at this time of night the highway up on the valley's side was empty of traffic. He saw the faint light of a single house a couple of kilometres away, then came to a smaller road marked *Underhill Farm Road—Private* by a faded sign that moved past his headlight. Might as well see if Cassie and Ivan were there. There was no point in going home, because home wasn't in this world. He took the turn and rode along a rougher dirt road that he was pretty sure didn't exist.

Everything was confusing. Ivan found it difficult to put events together enough to make sense of them. The old couple at the farm, the man waving a shotgun about rather wildly, and the woman trying to keep some control of the situation while she struggled as much as her husband to cope with events, were clearly the long-lost grandparents that Cassie had hoped for. Oddly, Reenie and Cal were already here. It was like a dream where things change fast and illogically and he could never quite work out what was happening. He felt giddy with confusion, fatigue and huge relief that he and Cassie had survived the journey on Sinclair's bike. Gran's car parked in the yard made him think she would appear too, before he saw the P plates and realized that Reenie must have been driving it. He watched the meeting between Cassie and the old people, silently.

The old couple bore an obvious family resemblance to Thistle, Cassie and Phil. The woman had the crazy hair and intense look, and the man the wiry build and abrupt manner. They looked dazed. Eventually, they invited everyone into the house, dogs calmed and gun put away. Mrs Redhill pulled out some blankets and pillows, gave them to Cassie and Ivan and said, "We'll talk in the morning. I'll make you a nice cocoa. You can sleep in Theodora's room with Reenie, and you can have the couch."

Wilfred stopped at the farmyard gate. Dogs barked and from behind a wall of dark trees he saw lighted windows, even though it was the middle of the night. Wilfred was wary of dogs. He'd never had one. He saw Sinclair's bike, and a small car of unfamiliar make in the driveway. He didn't know much about farms, but even to him it looked like a visitor's car; Reenie's, he guessed. Hoping the dogs were tied up, he dismounted his bike, and killed the engine, leaving the light on. He fumbled with the gate catch and wheeled the bike toward the house.

The dogs started barking again before anyone was settled. Mr Redhill looked at Ivan and Cassie, and said with the deadpan humour familiar to Ivan from previous observation of farmers round Willowvale, "The dogs are over-excited. I'd better take them round the back in case anyone else drops in."

Cal said, "I'll go with you," and they left the others in the sitting room. Mrs Redhill in her floral dressing gown and slippers said nothing, staring at Cassie drinking her cocoa as if she'd seen a ghost, the way she had done ever since Cassie came into the house.

CHAPTER TWENTY-TWO
RETURN TO THE OBSERVATORY

"So we go back to the observatory. I go home and get Thistle and Raven. Wilfred, Pip…" Cassie glanced at them and said no more. What Jess had said came back to her. Maybe it was true. Maybe she was bossy, as Jess said.

Vi and Herb found helmets for them. Cassie had an old equestrian helmet and Wilfred a plastic bike helmet from way before the disaster. Somehow he'd left the observatory without the two shiny helmets that matched his bike. The odd helmets were probably better than nothing… but not much; however they made the grandparents happier. Wilfred rode Sinclair's bike. Cassie, relieved, rode Wilfred's, which was easier to manage than Sinclair's. Reenie, expressing some misgivings about the road, nervous of scratches and flat tyres, drove her grandmother's car with Pip and Ivan as passengers.

They set out from the farm early, their stomachs filled with home-laid eggs. Vi insisted on lending Cassie and Ivan clean clothes. Cassie was in an outfit that wouldn't have looked too out of place at home, a pair of too-big jeans, rather worn, stiffly ironed into a crease and a t-shirt that had been Thistle's or perhaps Vi's once, with *Save the Franklin* printed on it, whatever that meant. Ivan wore a checked shirt of Herb's and some patched jeans held bunched up by a cracked leather belt. Vi and Herb— Cassie couldn't think of them as Granny and Grandpa or any names like that—waved them off into the perfect summer morning.

Wilfred led the way. They were a short distance up the Underhill road when he stopped.

Oh no. An accident. Someone lay beside the road. With a feeling of dread at what she would see, Cassie pulled up next to Wilfred. Reenie stopped the car nearby. Wilfred was already leaning over the person. A trail bike lay beside the road.

"It's Sinclair. What on earth is he doing here? How did he get into this world?"

"There's no blood."

Sinclair lay curled up as if he was in bed, except that he had his crash helmet on, with the visor down, and was lying beside a road.

Wilfred shook Sinclair's shoulder. "He's not dead. He's asleep."

Pip and Reenie came over. "That's my bike," Pip said.

Nobody had had time, or even thought, to explain to him about Sinclair.

Wilfred shook Sinclair again. He groaned and tried to sit up. He lifted the visor and Cassie saw that he was very pale. He was completely uninjured, leather jacket unscratched, no gravel marks on his jeans. Pip's bike, she was relieved to see, also showed no sign of damage. There were no skid marks and the bike lay beside the road as if someone had placed it there. Pip righted it and inspected it for damage without asking why Sinclair was there.

Sinclair sat unsteadily amongst the grass.

"What are you doing here?" Cassie asked.

"Going to O'Malley."

"You're in the wrong world," Wilfred said, still bending over Sinclair.

Cassie saw Wilfred step back, his hand on his jaw. Sinclair sprang up and before anyone knew what was happening, he jumped onto his own bike, the engine of which Wilfred had left running, and sped off in the direction of the highway and O'Malley after executing a tight U-turn that would have left an impressive cloud of dust if the morning hadn't been veiled in a thick dew.

Cassie, Pip, Reenie, Ivan and Wilfred stood in the road and watched until Sinclair disappeared round the nearest bend.

"That was weird," said Ivan.

"What's he doing here?" said Pip. Ivan, Pip, and Reenie wandered a little down the road, Ivan gesticulating as he told the strange tale of Sinclair's arrival at the observatory.

Wilfred took his hand from his face.

Cassie saw an angry red mark on his fair skin. "He hit you."

"It's okay."

"Let me look." Cassie put her hand on Wilfred's cheek. He blushed and flinched. "Does it hurt that much?"

"No."

"I can help. Let me look."

"No. Leave it."

Cassie felt hurt. "But Wilfred…" she touched his cheek gently again.

"Don't!" said Wilfred angrily and turned his back.

"I know first aid."

"Don't, Cassie. It makes it harder for me."

"I want to help."

"Don't you understand? Don't be nice to me. It doesn't help. I know you like Ivan best. If you're nice to me it—" he groaned "I can't explain. Work it out for yourself."

Cassie's hand dropped to her side and she felt herself blush too. "It's all so…complicated." She didn't know what to say, and couldn't speak anyway.

Wilfred jammed the ridiculous bicycle helmet onto his head and buckled it. "I shouldn't be here. I should have stayed with Jess."

Relieved at the change of subject, Cassie regained the power of speech. "Jess is big and mean enough to look after herself, and she's older than you. She should be worrying about you." Why was Wilfred saddled with all these poisonous relatives? Jess was much more interesting now than Cassie had previously thought, but still, she was self centred and abrasive. His mother, who Cassie had met during the adventure last winter, was the living end as far as stereotypical plastic O'Malley mothers went, and for Wilfred to suddenly find that the odious Rex Bagshaw was his father must be enough to shrivel his soul.

"I feel responsible for her. I shouldn't have left. Look what it achieved; a big fat nothing, except to let Sinclair loose on this world."

"Why? It's not your fault that he's here."

"Yes it is. He must have seen me get into this world and copied."

"How'd you get the bike into this world?"

"It was easy. I just went out there, brought it inside the house, and took it out at the right time. The hardest part was getting it up the step."

"So that flash-y, switch-y thing was still going on?"

"Yes. It's not so bad now that it's all to do with Jess and not at all the professor."

"What? Jess can control it?" Cassie was surprised.

Wilfred looked doubtful. "Sort of."

Cassie suddenly remembered that she was on her way to get Thistle and Raven and reunite them with Vi and Herb. "Anyway, that's neither here nor there. We have to get going. If you're sure you're okay."

"Yes. And no," muttered Wilfred.

Cassie wanted to hug him to make him feel better, but she thought it would be a bad idea, so she stood still, feeling foolish and confused. Something about this conversation made her feel sad in a way she had not experienced before.

Ivan came over to them, wary of getting drawn into their conversation. "Seeing as Sinclair took his bike and left Phil's, Cassie, we've decided you can come with us in the car. Phil wants to ride his bike." Cassie found the number of different names her brother seemed to have astounding. "Pip," she said.

"Yeah, him. Pip. Phil. Radcliffe. Reenie seems to call him Cal."

Cassie was happy enough to ride in the car. She was a bit tired of motorbikes. Pip's was okay, but riding Sinclair's with Ivan on the pillion had been a nerve-wracking experience that she was both relieved to have survived and proud to have achieved. She sat comfortably in the back of the little car that looked nothing like cars in O'Malley, and certainly not like the few cars in Willowvale, dozing and dreaming of her parents' reunion with their families.

When she woke they were driving up the last few hundred metres of the bumpy track that ended at the observatory. Cassie's mind was full of plans; how to break the news to Thistle and Raven; how to persuade them that the whole unlikely story was true; to take them to meet Vi and Herb; to search for Raven's family. The car stopped with a jerk. Ivan and Reenie got out, slamming the doors. Cassie came back from her thoughts and climbed out too. Ivan, Reenie, Pip and Wilfred waited for her in the driveway in front of the buildings.

"Something's different," said Wilfred.

"No, don't be silly." Cassie went to the door and knocked. A hollow echo sounded inside. They waited. "This door's always locked. Let's go round the back." They picked their way along the side of the building, over the weeds and broken glass. The back door was open. Flies buzzed in the porch. Cassie entered the kitchen. "Jess! Professor! We're back."

A burnt-out candle stood on the table; mugs and plates lay in the sink.

The books Jess had been so interested in were on the table; but everything was coated in a thick fuzz of dust. A chair lay on its side on the floor, and in the light fitting the bulb was blackened and smashed. Cobwebs draped the cornices.

"Jess? Professor Carter?"

"What is this place?" asked Reenie.

"Where are they?" said Ivan.

"It's the place where Thistle and Raven crossed from one world to the other," Cassie said to Reenie and Pip. "I don't understand. Where are Jess and the professor? They were here a few hours ago."

Everyone except Reenie and Pip thought at the same moment that Jess and the professor might be asleep. After all, it was still early. The sun was barely above the eastern hills.

The professor's room was empty, squalid; just a bed with mouldering grey blankets and a cupboard with its plywood door swinging open. How could she live like this? The second bedroom was worse, its curtain and glass jagged over the window cavity, and piles of dry leaves, rubbish and dead spiders in every corner.

"Jess! Professor!"

No answer.

"They must be in the observatory."

Cassie, Ivan and Wilfred had what in other circumstances would have been an amusing collision as they all tried to leave the room at the same time. They untangled themselves. Wilfred was first out, and was across the driveway and on the doorstep of the observatory by the time Cassie got outside.

"Oh."

Ivan, Reenie and Pip came up behind, nearly knocking her over because Cassie had stopped dead still.

"What's wrong?" said Pip.

Cassie, unable to speak for the second time that morning, pointed.

The observatory's blocky lower section was intact, though the window was broken and tall grass swept at the door. The dome, however, was a skeleton of metal ribs. Inside it, the ruin of the telescope peered pathetically at the sky.

Wilfred pounded the door, which opened under his hand as if someone was inside, but it was the slow action of rusty hinges and the catch giving way. Cassie saw him look inside. "No," he said. He went in. "Jess, where are you?"

Reenie and Pip inspected the fringes of the buildings. Cassie and Ivan were too shocked to do anything. Soon Pip and Reenie returned. "Are you sure this is the place? Nobody's been here for years," said Pip.

Wilfred came out of the observatory. "They've gone. It's as if Jess was never here."

"No!" Cassie said. "It can't be. It's a mistake." She ran to the back door and into the kitchen again. "There must be something, some clue. How are we going to get back?" She couldn't breathe properly. Everything had been working out like a solved puzzle. How could it all fall apart so spectacularly now? She started searching the kitchen, stirring up clouds of dust.

"What are you doing?" asked Reenie, who had followed her inside.

"They must have left a message, or a clue." Cassie sneezed.

"This professor and Jess? But Cassie, nobody's been here for ages. Look at the dust, the cobwebs."

Cassie felt sick. "It's our only way back. It was. And now Wilfred and I, and Pip, and Sinclair…are stuck. It's like when Raven and Thistle came. I'll never see them again." She clenched her fists so hard it hurt.

"We'll think of something," said Reenie.

"No, we won't. It's impossible." She looked around the bleak room. The professor's easel and telephones were still in the corner. The old journal and the astronomy book lay on the table under the dust, as if they'd been there last night, but years ago. She felt a tear slide down her cheek, and sneezed to hide it.

"Let's go outside. It's awful in here." Reenie put her arm around Cassie's shoulder.

Cassie wiped her nose on her arm and sneezed again, genuinely this time. "I should have known everything would turn to snake shit the moment I thought it was all falling into place." She allowed Reenie to steer her gently out of the house.

CHAPTER TWENTY-THREE
MOONRISE

So many explanations, so many arrangements. Now Cassie and Wilfred, stuck in Ivan's world, were as settled-in as could be expected.

Except that nothing was really settled. Cassie seethed with the frustrated wish to reunite her family, while Wilfred wilted with regret at leaving Jess and his mother separately ignorant of his location or indeed continued existence.

Although Ivan felt it was pointless, and suspected that the others did too, they spent every spare moment trying to work out a way into Wilfred and Cassie's world. They made a large, complicated spreadsheet with everything on it that they could think of, starting with drums in both worlds, sunset, the power poles, meteors, observatories and eccentric astronomers, and ending with ideas so wild and complex that even after writing them down, they had forgotten the reason for the idea by the time they looked at the spreadsheet again. They'd haunted the lookout where Ivan and Cassie first met, trying every possible idea, and then reluctantly went back to the ruined observatory with Reenie and Phil, and tried to see patterns in everything that could possibly fall into one.

Cassie and Wilfred settled uneasily into life in this Willowvale. School was okay, with both enrolled in the same year as Ivan under some special arrangement sorted by Ivan's parents. Cassie was the object of much admiration from every boy from year nine to twelve, and Wilfred, with a haircut forced on him by Mum, had emerged as an unlikely, distant heart-throb for every girl in the younger half of the school. They clung together a little, like survivors on a desert island, and Wilfred obsessively kept his perso-text charged and in working order, despite the impossibility of ever getting a connection on it.

Ivan felt somewhat left out until one day after a music class, when all the others had clattered out to lunch, Cassie picked up a school guitar and from its battered body brought forth a flood of music that Ivan had forgotten she had in her. He picked up another long-suffering music-room guitar and followed. It felt like coming home, to play again, and like a joyful reunion to make music with Cassie.

Wilfred came in and sat at a desk far back in the classroom. Ivan was barely aware of his presence, until a voice floated lightly over their improvisation, fitting wordlessly with the chords and melodies. Ivan and Cassie caught each other's glance and kept playing until their music drew gently to a natural end. Ivan held his breath and saw Cassie doing the same. Nothing happened at all for several seconds. Ivan became gradually aware of sounds outside the room; someone walking down the stairs, the shouts of kids playing handball outside, a crow calling, a truck changing gear in the street.

There were no plans. All those weeks of fruitless brainstorming had rendered Ivan, Cassie and Wilfred despondent about ever finding a way to connect with the world Wilfred and Cassie came from. None of them spoke of it, afraid of jinxing their chances of ever working it out; an unspoken joint superstition that everyone knew the others had, but nobody would mention.

It was a wet week, and although summer was barely over, the weather was cold. Ivan, Wilfred and Cassie went to Ivan's place after school, no-one talking about the spreadsheet that lurked reproachfully in Ivan's laptop, or the many improbable possibilities they should be investigating, but everyone thinking of them. Even Cassie was silent and discouraged. Ivan looked at her out of the corner of his eye. He wanted to hold her hand, put his arms around her, as he had in the green gully in the bush near the observatory when they met unexpectedly just a few weeks ago. But she was remote now. He thought she was angry, but he had no idea whether she really was, and if so, was she angry with the world, or circumstances, or with him?

Frankie, the Williams' dog, woke up and trotted into the sitting room. She nuzzled Ivan's knee, and made a sound that meant "give me attention." Absently, he stroked her.

There were voices at the door, and Mum, Ivan's young sister Anna and her friend Maddie came in.

"What are you lot doing? Just sitting?" Mum sounded puzzled and a bit exasperated. "I've got some people from the Domestic Violence Committee coming 'round for a meeting soon. If you're not going to make yourselves useful"—she included Wilfred and Cassie in this remark—"you'd better stop cluttering the place up and clear out. It's going to be complicated enough. Cassie, shouldn't you have caught your bus by now?"

Cassie was staying with Vi and Herb at Underhill Bend Farm, but this arrangement was less than ideal and involved long trips on the school bus into Willowvale every day. "I'm staying with Gran and Pop tonight," she said, meaning Ivan's grandparents. Wilfred was staying in Reenie's room until something happened. Which possibly meant he'd be there forever.

Wilfred stood up politely and said, "Sorry, Mrs Williams."

"Call me Elena, Wilfred, I wish you would."

Ivan and Cassie stood too, not wanting to get mixed up in the pre-meeting tidying nor in the meeting itself.

"You could take Frankie for a walk," said Mum, "unless you'd rather mow the lawn or go and study."

Ivan went to get Frankie's lead. A walk sounded like a good idea. He and Wilfred waited with Frankie on the front path.

Anna and Maddie came out. "Cassie says she'll catch up," they told Ivan and Wilfred.

Frankie was impatient but slow, so they set off on her usual route up the hill and into the scattered bush of the ridge that overlooked the town.

Ivan and Wilfred walked slowly, pausing frequently to wait while Frankie sniffed a stump or marked her territory on a tree. They were near the water tanks at the top of the ridge when Cassie caught up. She was laden with a picnic rug and a large bag.

"Your mother is in full flight getting things sorted. I think she's got about twenty people coming. We're having a picnic for dinner. I've got everything."

"Okay," said Ivan, still feeling flat and unaccountably hopeless.

"Come on," said Cassie. She and Wilfred went ahead. Ivan let Frankie finish her investigation of an interesting smell and followed.

"Why do you want to have a picnic here?" They were at the place where the power lines crossed the ridge. The long sweep of their first span swooped past the trees and down the valley. Clouds sat moodily over the next ridge—the one where the sun used to set so meaningfully, but where now it just went down every evening.

"I like it here."

They'd been to this place many times in the last month. Ivan didn't want to hang around up here. It reminded him of their failure to find a way through, and of the thought that perhaps one day they would find a way and he'd never see them again; a thought that filled him with desolation. Phil (or Radcliffe, Pip, or Cal), seemed happy in this world, but Ivan knew Cassie would not be content until she'd reunited her parents with the wider family, and he didn't know if she would be happy here without them.

They ate perched on a boulder poised at the brink of the valley. The scene was peaceful, and its ordinary calm filtered delicately into Ivan. After the last crust had been fed to Frankie and the last of the lemonade drunk, they sat quietly, facing west.

"I still can't believe that we'll never get back. I'm going to keep trying forever."

Clouds hung over the western ridge. They seemed to say, don't bother looking this way for answers. Don't even try. Ivan couldn't stand it. Nothing was going to happen, no matter what they did. Uncomfortable again with the place, remembering his first meeting with Cassie, half wishing he was alone with her now, feeling mean because despite the simmering rivalry between him and Wilfred over Cassie, Wilfred was his good friend too, Ivan took Frankie and wandered away from the others. He found himself entering the steep gully that ran from the lookout to the valley, where in another existence Raven and Thistle were as desperate to know what had happened to Cassie as long ago their own parents had been to know about them. He stumbled aimlessly over rocks, noticing odd details like an unusually coloured stone and an ancient soft-drink can. Water trickled down the gully and Frankie went to drink. Ivan idly put his hand into a small pool that was usually a sandy hollow. The water was cool and the feel of it on his hand was pleasant.

Something caught Ivan's attention. How could people dump rubbish in the bush like that? What was it? He went to investigate. Curved, painted wood, old and battered, smashed into several pieces, with some unpleasantly rotting fabric or leather, like parchment, attached torn and mouldy to its rim. A few rusty metal fittings, brackets with bolts. A drum.

Ivan froze. A drum? Why was a drum here? The hairs on the back of his neck stood up. Gingerly he picked the object up and inspected it. He could have sworn he'd seen it before; that it was the old curfew drum from Cassie's Willowvale. But how could it be? Was something happening? He shook his head to dislodge the thought. Nothing could happen. The drum in Cassie's world was destroyed, and no-one could use it again. The observatory was a ruin and Professor Fenella Carter long gone, as if she'd never existed. Sinclair had disappeared like a ghost into the city of O'Malley or further to oblivion. It was stupid to even try to get through. Maybe when he got back to the lookout Cassie and Wilfred would be gone because they'd never existed outside his dreams.

Frankie shook water off her muzzle, spraying Ivan with droplets. Ivan was jolted from his morose thoughts and had a strange feeling similar to the one he felt when an exciting new chord sounded unexpectedly; like a flower opening in a time-lapse film. The drum felt lifeless and repulsive. He dropped it where it had lain. As he returned to the lookout, between the tall boulders and trees that guarded the approach, he heard music. They were still there. They were real. Cassie had brought the ukulele that was neglected at home until her arrival. She played one of her wistful other-worldly songs. The simple sounds of the ukulele's nylon strings fell through the feather leaves of the forest like the last drops of water from a rainstorm. Wilfred sat on the picnic boulder, looking out over the valley.

The sun was hidden behind clouds and nothing had changed. That old drum was probably not even a drum. Ivan sat near Cassie and watched her play. She made a beautiful picture in the blue dusk, her hair a cloud around her head and even her blue and white school uniform a fitting part of the scene. The music floated around them, twisting with the erratic dance of small moths that fluttered around a white-flowering bush and the sound of the last quiet calls of the daytime birds.

To the west, clouds filled the sky, heavily on the ridges; but to the east, where night was already falling, the sky cleared with all the drama of stage curtains opening. Trees were like flat layers of scenery pieced though to show the sky behind. Through them Ivan saw the moon venture an edge over the horizon, growing steadily. Wilfred started to sing, embellishing the music from Cassie's ukulele. Ivan felt hypnotized. He stayed completely still, Frankie lying on his feet, the dog his only anchor to the ordinary world of school, parents, and the future, whatever that should be. This was one perfect moment that he would always remember, whatever happened.

Cassie looked up from the ukulele and although her face was in shadow,

Ivan knew she smiled at him. Frankie sighed and twitched in a dream of running. A kookaburra let out one comfortable chuckle as if to say, that's right.

It sounded like a cricket. A high chirp nearby. Ivan barely heard it at first, but soon the sound coalesced into a regular pattern; not quite a tune, but almost. Cassie kept playing.

Behind Ivan, Wilfred made an inarticulate sound of surprise and stopped singing. Ivan heard a whirring sound, and Wilfred took something from his pocket. A tiny red light glowed in his hand.

The moon separated itself from the eastern hills with majesty, a shining white disc larger than Ivan thought was possible, filigreed behind a lacing of branches and leaves.

"He'll reply this time."

"Why have you dragged us to this god-forsaken hillside?"

"Stop complaining, please. We're only one kilometre from town."

"Can you all be quiet for a moment? Something is different."

Cassie brought her music to a stop. Wilfred was a static silhouette. Frankie woke and leaned on Ivan's leg. Something crashed in the bush nearby. Ivan stood, picking Frankie up in his arms.

"I heard something up there."

"Give me a hand. These shoes will be ruined. Wait—"

The beam of a torch with a worn battery flitted across leaves and the voices approached. Around the nearest boulder came Jess, followed by Thistle and Raven. Everyone was surprised but Jess, Thistle and Raven more so than Ivan, Cassie and Wilfred.

"I heard Mum. Berenice. Where is she?" said Wilfred from within Jess' bear hug.

Berenice was nowhere to be found. She had not come through whatever strange doorway had briefly opened.

Wilfred's perso-text beeped, flashed and whirred again. A long string of messages printed inexorably onto his precious perso-tape. He held it up to the moonlight and read out loud, "Wilfred, I love you." Over and over. "Mum," he said.

Jess shook his arm. "Reply, quick! She might still get it. Tell her—it was the music—tell her, quickly. The connection might linger."

EPILOGUE

Ivan stood in the dappled shadows holding the dog in his arms like a baby. His phone buzzed in his pocket. He put Frankie down to answer it.

"Reenie. How's it going?" he said automatically, thinking as he spoke how peculiar it was the way social conventions rose to the surface even in the most surreal circumstances.

"Good. Look, Ivan, something weird's happened." Reenie was so keen to speak that Ivan couldn't get a word in to tell her what was happening at his end.

"Is it about Jack?"

"No, nothing like that." Reenie and Jack had become friends, and Jack let drop titbits of family history from time to time, which Reenie passed on to Cassie. "I've got this new lecturer." Reenie was studying a science degree, and had lectures in many disciplines of science during this first semester. "Astronomy. He's called Martin St Clare. He looks exactly like that Sinclair guy. He isn't him, but he's like his identical twin. A doppelganger."

"There are lots of people in the world who look a bit similar," said Ivan cautiously.

"I've been to the other world, Ivan. There are people the same. But listen. Sinclair's here too. He follows this Martin St Clare guy. I've seen him twice, in the lecture hall. He looks terrible. Sick. Like a shadow..."

"...and?" asked Ivan.

"I didn't want Sinclair to recognize me...he's a bit scary. I got one of my friends, Sally, you haven't met her, she's pretty tough, to talk to him. She thinks he's got a mental illness. He kept saying that he should have

Martin St Clare's job, and it wasn't fair. Then he just fell fast asleep right there in front of Sally, in the middle of the quad. He would have fallen flat on his face if he wasn't sitting down. Sally called me over. It was definitely Sinclair, but he looked awful. Then Martin St Clare came past. He looked annoyed, and said that Sinclair's been following him, stalking him. We have to help. If anyone can deal with Sinclair, it has to be us." Ivan heard Phil in the background saying something to Reenie.

This was the moment for Ivan to get a word in. "You'll never guess what I've got to tell you," he said.

www.ingramcontent.com/pod-product-compliance
Lightning Source LLC
Chambersburg PA
CBHW060602190726

48283CB00003B/1117